DEEP WATER

Letters from the Past

TINA CLOUGH

DEEP WATER

Copyright © Tina Clough 2023

The author asserts her moral right to be identified as the author of this work.

PAPERBACK ISBN 978-1-99-118716-1

A catalogue record of this book is available from the National Library of New Zealand

Lightpool Publishing

www.lightpoolpublishing.com

Cover and book design by Andrene Low

Chapter 1

On that breezy, late summer morning, with the early sun casting dancing tree shadows across the carpark, there was no indication of what was to come. No hint that a minor episode that day, would be the starting point of a sequence of events which would culminate in Emma's entire life changing in ways she could never have foreseen.

The library was always a space to treasure first thing in the morning, a time she particularly enjoyed. Staff moved about quietly doing the tasks that formed their pre-opening routines and only occasionally exchanged a few words, then the chatter in the staff room over a cup of coffee before they opened the doors at half past nine and the busy day began.

Emma was putting returned books back on the shelves, concentrating on endlessly repeating small segments of the alphabet silently in her head as she located the right place for each book, while at the same time she tried not to think about a maths assignment she had started on last night. The way her studies created a background rumble of ideas and thoughts, while she replaced books and did other morning tasks, was a constant factor in her life now. Thinking about maths and physics was turning into a bad habit, but ever since she decided to resume her interrupted studies extramurally the habit had crept up on her.

'Coffee time!' called Cora from behind the next block of shelves, so Emma replaced another couple of books before she left her trolley where it was and headed across the open space by the main entrance to get to the staff room. Glancing at the glass doors to the forecourt she saw two women already waiting for the library to open and though they were fifteen minutes too early, she felt guilty about ignoring them. I should have taken the trolley, so I looked busy, she thought, and then she laughed at herself. Those women knew very well that they were early and probably enjoyed their conversation.

'What were you doing out there? Did I leave some returned books behind?' she asked Cora, who was opening a new packet of biscuits with her teeth, a habit Emma found repulsive but never commented on, as Cora was touchy and quick to take offence.

Next time we need a new packet, she thought as she filled her mug, I'll dive into the cupboard and get one out before she does, and I'll open it with my fingers, show her it can be done – but without pointing it out, of course.

'No, just doing a quick survey of disintegrating spines,' said Cora and took a biscuit. 'We've not got many books on the for-sale shelf at the moment, so I thought I'd have a look and I found about two dozen that should have been weeded out ages ago. A couple of them might interest you – from the maths and science shelves.'

'I must have a look,' said Emma and picked her own biscuit from the middle of the packet. 'That old physics book I bought a few months ago was so funny, from the age when they filled in complicated tables of figures by hand and calculated averages and things by using those old hand-cranked calculators – all the things we never think of now, we just feed data into spreadsheets.'

Anne, who had been at the library longer than anyone, including Cora, studied Emma with a thoughtful expression and said, 'Why *did* you became a librarian when your head is always full of science and maths? I've been going to ask you for ages because it seems so counter intuitive. First training as a librarian and then doing a science degree - very unusual.'

'Oh, just one of those things,' said Emma casually, not wanting to be labelled either a freak or a show-off. 'I've always loved books and reading, so right from the time I was seven or so I thought working in a library would be heaven. I'm sure the staff at the

Tauranga library got sick of me sneaking in behind the counter to tell them about some book I was reading. But I'm also interested in maths, so I'm doing the degree more or less for fun. I started it some time ago and let it lapse, but now I'm serious about it, I want to complete it.' She winked at Anne and added, 'And I don't like loose ends and unfinished business.'

'Oh, for God's sake, you're not going to drag out the story about the jumper, are you?' Anne turned the others. 'I might as well tell you myself and spare her the trouble – I can see she's dying to tell you. A while back Emma came over for a cup of coffee on a Saturday morning, and my son Ethan said something sarcastic about me and knitting. And then the story unravelled – pun intended – and Emma found out that when I learnt to knit I started on a sweater for him, and now it's in a bag in the linen cupboard, half finished.'

'Well, so what?' said Cora. 'Nothing shameful in that, is there?'

'That's what I thought,' said Emma. 'Until Ethan told me she started it when he was three and now he's fifteen, and it's still not finished, so he uses it whenever he wants to embarrass his mother.'

'I couldn't do it – extramural studies need such focus,' said Cora when the comments about unfinished projects died down. 'Not only wouldn't I have the persistence to do it, but I don't' have the brains for it either. Maths tests always made me go into panic mode at school. And my husband would complain if I spent my evenings studying – he likes company on the sofa.'

'But don't forget,' said Anne, who had developed a solid friendship with Emma, though she knew little about her background, because they mostly talked about books and films, and sometimes about Anne's boys. 'Emma lives on her own, so she can spend as much time on her studies as she wants to – *and* she's got focus.'

And then the conversation at their end of the table blended in with that at the other end, and Emma's mind reverted to the maths problem and took no part in the discussion about the summer sales, which was the dominant topic until it was time to open the doors.

It was only just before they were closing that afternoon that Emma remembered to have a look at the books for sale and bought three for a dollar each, two novels and an old book by GH Hardy, a mathematician she had recently read a short article about on a website devoted to pioneers in the field.

Walking home in the pleasant summer evening made Emma feel vital and alive. She clutched her three bargain books against her chest with one arm, keeping her shoulder bag from swinging by holding it in place with her elbow and remembered her grandfather telling her that 'sitting up straight, walking with your head back, and swinging your arms is what makes us different from the apes'.

What a character he was, she thought as she side-stepped a group of teenagers coming towards her in a tight cluster, hogging nearly the whole width of the sidewalk. Her grandfather had been a self-educated working man who took pride in attending adult education classes in subjects he was interested in, like mathematics. When he died, Emma was thirteen and the only child or grandchild of his who had inherited his interest in maths. When she won the prize for the best essay in her year, aged eleven, he was so proud of her achievement, because writing on the topic of "what I like leaning most" she had written about maths. She smiled at how she had chosen to focus on maths because and written that "maths plays a part in every aspect of life." Her grandfather gave her a five-dollar bill and told her that using the word aspect in an essay at her age was very good, but what he liked best was that she chose maths to write about.

The twenty-five-minute walk to and from the city centre every working day was a calm interlude between work and home, a time to let her mind drift from one topic to another, unfettered by her innate sense of logic, which was always present when she talked to someone. Today was no exception and her mind moved seamlessly from worrying about a half-finished assignment to what she would have for dinner and from there to her father's surprising new life in Cairns. Now and then she glanced towards the western horizon where clouds towered up above the mountain ranges and thought she must check the forecast in the morning and avoid the mistake she made a couple of weeks back when she didn't check and got caught in a downpour halfway home without an umbrella. But inevitably her thoughts reverted to the papers she was doing in this final year of her degree. She already regretted cramming in more papers than she needed, because now assignments were lining up. Everything started with a rush this year, she thought as she climbed the stairs. I must make sure I keep up with everything and don't end up with any incomplete papers to finish next year.

When she sat down after dinner in her favourite blue armchair with the three books she had bought she told herself she would only have a quick look and then pick up her physics books. The top book in the little pile was *The Camomile Lawn*, a book she knew was famous; a first novel that became a best-seller and made the author instantly famous at the age of seventy. She had read *Wild Mary*, Mary Wesley's biography, but now realised that she hadn't followed up and read any of her novels. Putting the other two books back on the round table beside her chair, she opened *The Camomile Lawn* and was soon lost in the story, all thoughts of study forgotten.

Chapter 2

Two weeks later, after a period of intense work on
a maths assignment which clashed with two
other pieces of work that were due at more or less the
same time, Emma finally sat down in the middle of one
sleepless night with the old maths book she had bought
at the library. It had sat on the table beside her
armchair, along with the old copy of The Camomile
Lawn while she spent most of her free time at the
dining table with her laptop and textbooks or went
running to give herself some energy.

She had woken up at midnight after an hour's
sleep, from an old dream that sometimes returned to
haunt her, and which still had the power to leave her
too disturbed to go back to sleep. Standing in the
kitchen waiting for the water to boil for a cup of tea,
she wondered if this happened to others who
experienced intense loss and grief. It's like a rewind of

time, she thought, as if somehow my mind reverts to the past, as if it needs to remind me of what it was like at the time. So immediate seeming and vivid that it takes time to get over, even when I wake up and realise it was a dream.

With a mug of tea on the table beside her armchair, she looked up GH Hardy on her phone, to remind herself of what he had done and read about his achievements, before she opened the book. His life work was impressive, but what particularly stood out was the principle that was named after him and another man, which was still a valuable tool in population genetics more than a hundred years later. She smiled at Hardy quoted as describing his revolutionary mathematical solution as 'very simple'.

The slightly stained book smelled musty and had cracks in the spine, so supporting it on her thighs to avoid damage she opened it carefully. Someone had written a note on the flyleaf, a scribbled ballpoint pen note saying that it had been donated by 'along with other books about mathematics by the family of the owner'. Cryptic, thought Emma, when they omit the name of the person who originally owned it or the family. The note was unsigned and undated and might have been left unfinished by mistake, thought Emma, as she studied the handwriting and thought it was probably Anne's. Or perhaps there had been a boxful of books and by the time she got to that particular one she was so tired of writing that note in the front of each one that she left out the details by mistake.

On the reverse side of the flyleaf the name Hermann S was written in ink in an old-fashioned, or perhaps a slightly foreign looking style of handwriting. The book was published in nineteen-forty-one, so maybe it had been bought by Hermann reasonably soon after that and at that time, he would of course have used a fountain pen. An hour later, when Emma's eyes were nearly closing by themselves, she stopped reading and flicked idly through the rest of the book before putting it away and going back to bed. The pages flickered past in an even stream until nearly at the end of the book when an envelope fell out. She picked it up and looked at the stamp depicting a tuatara lizard and thought how these days she hardly ever saw postage stamps and found it hard to picture what was on them. The envelope was addressed to Mr Harry Webber and the sender's name on the back of the envelope was Gerald Miller, who lived in Seaview Road, Remuera, Auckland.

Wide awake again, Emma opened the flap and was delighted to find a letter inside, handwritten in a style similar to the name on the flyleaf, with a slightly unusual way of forming some letters. The letter was dated 4 December 1991 and started 'Dear Hermann' which was interesting and woke Emma up. Why was the name on the envelope different from the name at the top of the letter? The handwriting confirmed that both had been written by the same person, and at the end the writer signed off with the name Gerhart, also different than that on the back of the envelope.

After reading the letter Emma sat for several minutes absent-mindedly looking into the distance. If the ideas that had formed in her mind were right, then what she had in her possession could potentially cause havoc with the local authority elections in October, and significantly damage the hopes of one of the Auckland mayoral candidates. Mentally warning herself about making assumptions, she decided to do a bit more digging on the Internet to see if she could find some concrete evidence.

In the letter, Gerhart/Gerald said he hoped the GH Hardy book, which he had found in a second-hand bookstore, would be of interest "to someone as mathematically interested as you are", and he hoped it had arrived in time for Hermann/Harry's birthday. He then went on to cover news about his family, and particularly mentioned his twelve-year-old grandson and namesake, whom he said he often took for excursions on his boat. He wrote that he was continuing to use his and Gerald junior's fishing trips to educate him about things he should know and their topic at the moment was the proven supremacy of the white race, the necessity to keep "white men untainted by colour or other race's characteristics" and the moral duty of respectable men to uphold traditions. He briefly referred to his disappointing son, Karl, who had rejected his own strongly held values and "sold out", and how much he looked forward to introducing young Gerald to the Brotherhood in a few years.

Gerald Miller was the name of the wealthy man in Auckland, who many months out from the elections had already become a familiar name in the press by voicing opinions on current topics and working hard on becoming a well-known name. But was he really the man written about as a twelve-year-old in that letter from 1991? From obscurity and a quiet life, Mr Miller had sprung into the public consciousness in what Emma thought was a well-orchestrated campaign, probably managed by PR consultants. A man with no previous experience in politics, who had all the attributes of a perfect, conservative mayoral candidate. He was already outlining his plans for what he would do if he became the mayor of Auckland, so if there was a connection to the white supremacist man who wrote the letter, it was very interesting. She was acutely aware of the various implications of what she had found, not least the risk of being sued by a man who just by chance had the same name. She picked up her notebook and made a list of things to look up, put everything away and went back to bed.

The next day was her rostered-off Saturday, and she picked up the notebook while she was having breakfast to remind herself of what she had written in the night: find out who Gerald Miller's parents and grandparents are, find out how he became wealthy, find out what the Brotherhood was and if it still existed, find out everything possible about Hermann and Gerhart, though the only clue to Hermann's surname was the letter S on the flyleaf of the book.

Saturday mornings were usually devoted to cleaning the flat and doing laundry, but her quest had become irresistible, so Emma sat down in her PJs to devote the morning to more interesting things than housework before her lunch date with Fletcher. She booted up her laptop and started searching, but she soon had to admit it seemed unlikely that the present-day Gerald Miller had anything to hide. His parents were Karl and Louise Miller, both still alive and living in Auckland where Gerald was born. He went to school there and married a girl from Hamilton, who was attractive and very thin in the way of obsessive women, who push the food around on their plates, pretend to eat and leave most of it. Emma was very familiar with this style of pretend-eating; her friend Catriona had for a long time been one of those women, and it was only when her twins were born that she started eating like normal people.

'Let's face it,' Catriona had said late one evening on Skype. 'I'm breastfeeding twins and I'm hungry all the time, and if I don't eat, I run out of steam. I'm so tired a lot of the time I don't give a shit what I look like, so long as I can have another coffee and a couple of biscuits.'

Emma closed her laptop and spent an hour doing

housework, still in her PJs, before she finally got dressed and walked into town to meet Fletcher, but all the while her thoughts revolved around Gerald Miller. It could easily be a coincidence that his grandfather's name was the same as his, it was not unusual to pass on names within a family, but that his father's name was Karl, the same name mentioned in the letter was interesting. She had found nothing even vaguely suspicious about his grandfather, who had immigrated from England, arrived in New Zealand in his mid-thirties and married a local woman, who was the daughter of a suburban car dealer. Emma knew how easy it would be to leap to conclusions and warned herself against confirmation bias. The fact that it would be exciting to unearth secrets about a wealthy and rapidly more prominent candidate was irrelevant.

Chapter 3

The walk from the flat into town made Emma realise that the end of summer was close. Last night's cloud banks had vanished, and though the day was sunny, the wind was chilly. She buttoned her new jacket right up to the neck and put the collar up.

Fletcher always picked the same café to meet, and even suggested it when she said they could meet at her place.

'It's not that I don't think your flat is lovely, and I know you make gorgeous coffee with that lovely machine you bought, but I like the Little Coffee House,' he said when she asked him why. 'I spend my life in a luxury lodge where everything is expensive and substantial and minutely curated — believe it or not, that's what they call it. Even my house out there is of the same standard, and everything in it matches the décor in the lodge itself — I can't get away from it. God forbid we would tolerate a minutely scratched table or a cracked saucer or pillowcases that don't match the sheets. The Little Coffee House is cosy and casual, and I like the way they have random mugs of different designs, I always hope I'll get one of the old Temuka mugs, the white and brown ones from whenever it was – eons ago. They've got the perfect handles, not too big and not too small.'

Now Emma laughed at her high school friend, who despite his protestations and his appearance when he was off duty, was the manager of the exclusive Mountain View Lodge, halfway up the foothills to the real mountains, forty-five minutes out of town. Dressed in jeans and a scruffy sweatshirt with the faded logo of an American university on the front, he was unrecognisable from polished image she had seen in photos from the lodge.

'This is interesting,' she said when she hugged him and felt the stubble against her cheek. 'You must have something big on tomorrow and for the next few days. Anything interesting? Anyone famous?'

'Have you turned into Sherlock Holmes? How the hell did you know?' Fletcher sat down and looked hard at her. '*Please*, don't tell me it's been leaked! We're supposed to keep it under tight wraps until their publicists releases the official press statements next week. If nothing's written about it in connection with the lodge before they release the photos, we get an enormous bonus payment.'

'I know nothing at all – don't worry, Fletch! I made an educated guess based on the stubble and you being off on a Saturday, which is unusual for you, so something special must mean you can't leave the golden cage for your usual Monday or sometimes Tuesday. I can't remember ever having lunch with you on a Saturday before.'

He looked relieved and impressed in equal parts. 'Very smart! And you're right. The whole place is booked out for a party lasting five days, starting tomorrow lunchtime with the arrival of the couple about to be married on Tuesday, believe it or not. Their schedules are insane, and apparently Tuesday is the perfect day for some crazy reason. Guests arrive on Monday, eighty all up, and then there's a pre-wedding dinner, then a massive wedding banquet, an eight-piece band flown in from the US, dancing, champagne fountain, dancers flown in from LA choreographed by Paris Goebbles, the lot.'

He laughed and shook his head. 'And not only that, but we'll be flat out managing all the hangers-on as you can probably imagine. Security people, personal assistants, hairdressers and so on. Apart from a couple of security guys, who have to stay at the lodge, the rest will be commuting from hotels in town, so we're running shuttle vans to and from motels and hotels. But marvellous PR for us and we make a very impressive profit.'

'Who is it?' asked Emma casually as if it didn't

really matter, and Fletcher chuckled. 'Oh no, you're not getting me to tell you by mistake – all I can say is that the couple is so famous even my grandma will know who they are. After this lunch I drive straight back, shave and get my suit on and act like the perfect luxury lodge manager I'm paid to be. Lots of preparations under way, the place is crazy – delivery vans everywhere. I just needed a few hours away from the bustle.'

They chose the same lunch, a stack of corn fritters with tomato relish, followed by the doughnuts the café was famous for. 'Why are we so boring? We always have this,' said Emma. 'Every time we meet here I think that *this* time I'll order something else, and then I hear you order corn fritters and a doughnut, and I can't help myself.'

'This year we'll celebrate your birthday with dinner at the lodge and you can dress up and have anything you like, as long as you don't ask for corn fritters – not that we have them on the menu. Remember your first birthday here when you turned thirty-one and you'd just moved into your flat a few months before - we went out for a Thai dinner. This time it will be very upmarket, and you can have a room and stay the night, get the whole experience.'

'What a great present, thank you! It's lucky for me you aren't married, or these things might never happen. You're an asset in my life, you really are.'

'Remember that guy I went out with for a few

months last year? And the one the previous year, the one I met when I went skiing? The minute they find out what my job is like, and how I have no control over my life, they can't say goodbye quick enough. I'm kind of married to the job and the place.'

He didn't seem to mind, but Emma realised she had never thought of this and wondered how much he did mind. 'I'm sorry, Fletcher – do you worry about it?'

'God no! I'm probably not cut out for domestic bliss, anyway. And though the job is very restricting I get paid an indecent amount of money to do it. But have a look at this!'

He handed her his phone and sat back. 'Start the video and you'll see a complete walk-through of the place. I made it especially for this couple who're getting married on Tuesday. They wanted to see how it looks as you walk in and through the whole place, not just stills and little video snippets like on the website. I had to do it four times to get it right. The last part is one of our premium suites – the one the bridal couple will have.'

'My God, it's stunning – that suite and the bathroom!' said Emma when she had watched it twice. 'And the foyer or whatever you call it with the huge stone fireplace and groups of brown leather armchairs and brass lamps – very classy, like an Edwardian gentlemen's club. And views to die for. Are those real stag's heads?'

An hour and a half later she walked away after

turning down Fletcher's offer to drive her home and thought how lucky she was to have been friends with him since childhood. Having dinner at the lodge was a treat of the kind she might never be able to afford or want to spend money on. She walked fast up the hill to counter the chilly wind and thought of how the move south had transformed her life in a positive way after trauma and grief, and how lucky she was compared to a lot of people.

I'm happy here, she thought, truly happy. My flat is lovely, I'm not in debt and the car will last another few years, that's all I need in life.

Emma unlocked the door to the flat, hung her jacket up and hesitated only a moment before she decided that despite how interesting her research was, the washing must get done. But her mind was so focused on the search for information about the Miller clan, that even as she turned the washing machine on she was lost in thought about more avenues to pursue, and nearly forgot to put the laundry powder in.

She got the letter out again to re-read the sentence about Karl, the disappointing son, and sat with the letter in her hand looking without focus out the window as she tried to work out how it might hang together in some logical way. She went through it in her mind; was it two stories or one? On the one hand there was the grandfather who had a son called Karl and left a fortune to his grandson, on the other hand a possibly German immigrant posing as English, who had a son called Karl he didn't approve of and a grandson he was grooming. Two separate-seeming stories, and maybe not enough to link them, but there were some striking similarities. Admittedly there must have been lots of men called Gerald Miller in the last few decades, but Emma felt that the specific mention of sons and grandsons nearly ruled out coincidence. Thinking back to what she knew about the period before the second world war, she realised that there were many people in England who openly sympathised with the Nazis, so maybe the German connection was a red herring. But the man who signed himself Gerald on the back of the envelope had signed the letter Gerhart, and the man he sent it to, was called Harry on the envelope was Hermann inside the letter; she continued to feel nearly certain her theory was right. So many pieces of the jigsaw and so many overlapping pieces of evidence, she thought, and they all seem to lead to the same conclusion, but to prove it beyond doubt I need more. I need one crucial fact that can't be dismissed as coincidence, a keystone to lock together this arch of supposition. If I told anyone my theory now, they'd probably say it's just coincidence on a major scale, the kind of thing that happens now and then.

Googling the mayoral candidate's grandfather brought up a variety of articles from when he died in 2008 at the age of ninety-four. The New Zealand

Herald had a long obituary that portrayed him as a "superbly gifted" businessman, who had arrived from England in 1950, married a local girl and amassed a fortune. He started out on borrowed money and set up a manufacturing plant to make turbines for power stations at the time when electricity generated by dams and hydro-lakes was becoming big business. Then he expanded his range, began exporting his products and made a fortune. His social life was also mentioned, ski holidays with a prime minister, golf with mayors and once with a visiting royal. His fiftieth birthday party was described as an extravagant show of wealth, and the house he bought in Seaview Road in Remuera was for some time famous locally. Photos of it showed a big two-storied house, to which Miller had added a three-storied octagonal tower at one corner, where he kept his big Zeiss telescope in the room at the top. On a more personal note, one article mentioned that he was fond of music and fishing, a hobby he shared with his grandson and namesake.

'Yay!' said Emma out loud. 'It *is* the man who wrote to his friend about white supremacy and the mysterious Brotherhood. Fishing with his grandson – that's the last bit of proof I need, it can't possibly be a coincidence, it's the man who wrote the letter.'

Next she went to the National Library's website *Paperspast* with digitised New Zealand newspapers from close to a hundred years, a site she often recommended to those who came to use the computers at the library to research early immigrants or old family connections. By searching for Gerald Miller, in all newspapers between 1949 and 1951 she found him in a few minutes. An article in the Dominion, which seemed to be part of a series of articles about recent arrivals, came up with the Miller's name highlighted in yellow. It mentioned not only Gerald Miller, but also his friend Harry Webber, who both arrived on a ship from Argentina. They had been briefly interviewed about their plans in their new country along with another three passengers. 'Harry Webber!' said Emma out loud to herself, 'the man the letter was addressed to, it all fits!'

Argentina rang a bell too and quick check on Wikipedia confirmed her memory of how large numbers of Nazis escaped to that country along so-called Ratlines, escape routes set up before the end of the second world war; another link that supported her theory.

Of all the things she had discovered, the still unexplained organisation called the Brotherhood, was the most interesting. An older man grooming a grandson to believe in the theory of white supremacy was one thing, but if the Brotherhood was an underground group of neo-Nazis that still existed, and if the present Gerald Miller was part of it, then it was crucial information. The potential impact of having a man like that as mayor of Auckland, provided he still held those views, would be unthinkable for the majority of voters, provided they knew about it. But from what she had read about extremists over the last couple of years, the implication of having this explosive piece of information was fraught with risk. She sat for a while trying to estimate that risk, wondering if she might be able to make her knowledge pubic without risking repercussions, and then the washing machine beeped.

Chapter 4

With the washing in the dryer, Emma resisted the urge to do more research instead of mopping the kitchen floor, her least appealing piece of housework this morning, but her mother called on What'sApp just as she was filling the bucket.

'Did you hear from Ash recently?' she asked. Emma could tell from her tone that she was annoyed and wondered what her little brother had done this time.

'No? Well, I did – twice in a couple of days!' exclaimed her mother. 'He wants money again, and I thought he might have asked you instead when I told him to get a job and stop asking me to support him. It's high time he grew up and took charge of his life instead of this constant begging for help, don't you think?'

'I totally agree, but he hasn't called me this time, or not yet,' said Emma and turned the hot tap off. 'Last time he asked me for money I did what you've just done - I told him I was sick of it, in no uncertain terms.' She laughed. 'What I actually said was, "stop being a lazy, entitled bum and get a fulltime job." I bet you can't guess what he said, he told me he didn't have *time* for a fulltime job because he'd lose form! Form! He's a medium grade surfer, for God's sake not a top performance athlete. And if he hasn't made it anywhere near the top by now, he'll never do it - he's been at it for years.'

'Was that enough? Or did he persist?'

'Oh, Mum,' said Emma, half rueful and half laughing. 'You won't believe it - I said something I've thought of saying so some many times before and never said! I told him that if he expects me to hold down a fulltime job, so I can subsidise his lazy, self-indulgent lifestyle, then he needs to think again, because I'm not giving him another cent.'

'Wow!' said her mum and laughed. 'Very staunch, and I've just a moment ago told him something very similar. He was furious and said I don't love him, and I always put him second after you. So, I told him you've never asked me to fund you, and maybe he should sit down and consider that instead of moaning. I'm glad we're on the same page with this. I thought he'd call you instead, but he probably won't. Maybe he'll even get a proper job if we can stick to our guns, and he'll be forced to take responsibility for himself.'

'I know,' said Emma, after thinking while she listened to her mother. 'But we caused this ourselves, don't you think? He's so many years younger than me, and we all spoilt him because he was so cute and curly and funny. We probably made him think there's always going be someone ready to pick him up and dust him off, and now he's twenty-three and he still thinks that. Talk about making a rod for our own backs.'

She listened with one ear to her mother telling her that the company she worked for was advertising for an IT manager, while at the same time speculating about Gerald Miller, and then she suddenly woke up to what her mother was saying.

'They advertised the position, a new position, and you didn't know? They didn't inform you and offer you the chance to apply! Aren't you in charge of IT as part of your job?'

'I am, and I did voice my disappointment that I hadn't been asked to apply or at least been informed before they advertised the new job, but they said the role isn't in my employment agreement, just something they've let me take on temporarily. For two years!'

Emma was outraged on her mother's behalf. 'They said they'd *let* you take it on? As if they were doing you a favour? I think you should do something about this. Catriona would know, she's got all this stuff at her fingertips.'

'Oh, don't worry, darling!' Her mother chuckled. 'I'm not as green as I'm cabbage looking, as my mother used to say. I did say I was surprised, and then the next day when I was in staff room I got the perfect opportunity. I managed to mention quite casually to Greg, the admin guy, that your friend is an employment lawyer just as the CEO had come in behind me. It's unusual for the CEO to get coffee for himself, so I couldn't resist.'

'And? There's something coming, I can feel it. What did you say to Greg and what happened next?'

'Oh, I just pretended I hadn't seen the big boss come in. I had my back to the door, and I just made out I was already in the middle of a conversation with Greg about it, as if I was explaining who Catriona was. I said, "oh yes, she is an employment lawyer but she's not my friend, she Emma's friend." Luckily Greg is a smart guy, so he didn't say anything to ruin things. But when the CEO walked out with his coffee, Greg laughed and said he'd nearly asked me what the hell I was talking about, and then he saw me wink at him. So, time will tell, but if they apologise or something like it, I'll ask for a pay increase, a big one.'

Emma smiled. 'Well done! Let me know what happens, both with Ash and the pay increase. And don't accept a token gesture! I've got to get going with the cleaning now, so I can spend the rest of the day studying.'

The conversation with her mother stayed in Emma's head for the rest of the day, and after dinner, when she imagined Catriona might have put the twins to bed, she texted and asked if they could talk as she needed some advice.

'Any time,' Catriona texted back. 'Twins asleep, Duncan snoring in front of Sky Sport, and I'm just reading.'

'What's up?' she asked a few minutes later when Emma called her on Skype. 'Advice? Are you in some kind of trouble at work?'

'No, it's mum – she's not in trouble, but I think she wants to draw a line in the sand with her company about how they're using and abusing her, so to speak.'

When she had outlined her mother's predicament, Catriona smiled. 'Classic!' she said. 'Happens all the time – people simply don't understand that by giving someone extra responsibilities, which weren't in their original employment agreement, they have in fact appointed them to an additional role in a way, unless they point out that it's temporary in written form - particularly if it kind of runs on and ceases to be truly short-term. And then they decide to make it new fulltime position and advertise it without first inviting the person who's already doing the job to apply. A lot of older bosses just don't get it – the world changed a couple of decades ago and they're still lumbering around in the junle with the other dinosaurs.'

'Could you call her when you have a moment, please? She'd love to talk to you – she always asks after you and the twins, and perhaps you could just give her a hint about how to go about this?'

'Of course, no problem.'

'And how are the twins?' She looked tired, and

Emma wondered if the twins were keeping her up at night still. 'Do they sleep better now?'

'They're fine at the moment and I'm just a bit exhausted because I'm pregnant again.'

'Are you kidding? How the hell did that happen?'

Catriona made a kissy face and smiled. 'Just the usual way, you know, we went to bed one night and Duncan edged over to my side and …'

'Stop right there! I don't need the biology lesson — but weren't you back on the pill? And how old are the twins?'

'I *was* on the pill and heaven knows what happened — maybe I missed one or two. The twins are ten months old next week and this next little thing is due when they're less than a year and a half. Three kids under two. I think we should sell that rental property we bought years ago and use the money to employ a nanny for a couple of years.'

'That makes sense,' said Emma. 'But thank goodness it's not twins again. They run in Duncan's family, don't they?'

Catriona made a hideous face. 'Yeah, right! Keep your finger crossed! Don't forget that we didn't know the twins were twins to start with, because when they did the first scan Rowan was hiding behind Seamus — which he still does, curls up behind him when they're having a nap in the cot together. Time will tell.'

. . .

For the rest of the evening, while Emma studied and made a half-hearted start on another assignment, her thoughts were on the past. She never got to talk about it, she realised, and that was like another loss, not being able to talk about it. It felt as if her family and her close friends had made a pact to never bring the subject up in case it upset her. And now she herself didn't know how to introduce it into conversations without feeling as she was asking for sympathy. Their careful avoidance of it had stifled her ability to say the words she felt were trapped in her mind, unvoiced and unheard. She often thought of it now that the grief had settled down and she could think rationally about it, but it might be too late to ever raise it again. Absentmindedly she doodled little drawings of stars in the margin of her textbook and after an unproductive half hour she closed the book and went to bed with her Kindle.

____

Chapter 5

____

At the library the staff's afternoon break never saw everyone in the staff rom at the same time, not like in the morning in that last quarter of an hour before they opened the doors. Today only Anne was there when Emma arrived, and while she got her coffee she said over her shoulder, 'You know that old book I bought the other day, the maths book Cora said she'd put on the for-sale shelf? It had a very interesting letter in it – from 1991.'

'Was it a love letter?' asked Anne. 'A love letter in a musty old maths book would be such a great find. I've always hoped I'd find one - a bit more exciting than a shopping list or a receipt from the supermarket.'

Staff often spotted the varied bits of paper people used as bookmarks left in the books, and readers returning books sometimes told them about something amusing they had come across. Emma was once handed a marriage certificate from 1928 someone had found in a Lee Child novel, and which was eventually returned to the family it belonged to.

'No, but it was interesting, a letter from a man in Auckland to a friend of his, the owner of the maths book' said Emma now. 'But it resonated with me – you know how I told you about that online article I read not long ago about neo-Nazi groups in Europe and how white supremacists are increasing all over the world, and their members are standing in elections without revealing their beliefs. The guy who wrote the old letter mentioned an organisation here in New Zealand called the Brotherhood.'

From behind her Cora said, 'I've heard about a group called the Brotherhood - or maybe I've read about it. Was it addressed to one of our readers?'

Anne raised her eyebrows at Emma at this strange request and said jokingly, 'Are you going to report them, Cora?'

'But did it have a name on it – you know who it was addressed to or who wrote it?' persisted Cora, as if Anne hadn't spoken.

Emma wished she could rewind time and start this from scratch, because now she was in a spot she couldn't easily get out of and regretted making the comment about the Brotherhood.

'I can't remember now who's who - of the writer and the guy he wrote to, I mean,' she said and tried to sound vague. 'Either Miller or Webber, I think. Or it might have been Webster.' Trying to make it sound uninteresting suddenly seemed like a good idea, and if she could have had more than a moment's notice, she would have come up with some alternative for Miller.

Damn! she thought. That name is so much on my mind now, it just popped out. I'll have to be a bit more careful just in case it's linked to who I think it is – I don't want to be sued for defamation.

Anne laughed. 'Whatever! As my kids say. You know that film I told you about, the one I said was the only truly good vampire film I'd ever seen? The old one from Sweden called, "Let the right one in"? Well, I've got another one for you now and Tilda Swinton's in it, fabulous! It's called "Only lovers left alive" and it's really a love story – it's on Apple. I love Tilda Swinton.'

'But I don't have Apple, unfortunately,' said Emma. 'So, I'll have to wait for it to pop up somewhere else, but vampire movies aren't really my ting – I think it's the fangs.'

After the break she walked slowly back to the checkout desk, with a feeling of mild unease that she had failed to keep those names out of the conversation. She had only mentioned the letter to Anne as a curiosity linked to the neo-Nazi movement they had talked about recently over coffee in town. If I'd been quicker, she thought, I could have made up some names, but I was taken aback by Cora's question and the tone of her voice. And why would it matter if one of our readers had fascist beliefs – probably dozens do.

The next morning Cora brought the subject up again when Emma came across her in the staff toilets. 'You know that letter you mentioned yesterday – how old did you say it was?'

And Emma realised that this might be an opportunity to reduce the likelihood of Gerald Miller's name becoming involved before she knew for a fact that the Brotherhood still existed. She pretended to think and looked blankly at herself in the mirror above the handbasin, then shook her head. 'I think it was written about 1990.'

'It would be interesting to see it – could you bring it in?'

This time Emma was prepared, and the perfect comment instantly formed in her head. 'I didn't think it was very interesting, so I chucked it in the rubbish,' she said casually, turned the taps off and reached for a paper towel. 'It's not as if we'd be able to give it back to anyone. I bet it had been in that old book since before it was donated to us.'

'Ah,' said Cora. 'That's OK then.' On that mysterious note she left, and Emma remained for a moment, thoughtfully looking at herself in the mirror and wondering what this rather strange conversation had really been about.

The question of why Cora had brought the subject up again revolved in Emma's head for the rest of the morning. Why had Cora asked to see the letter and wanted more details? And why did she say "That's all right then" when Emma told her she'd thrown the letter away? Did she have a connection to some group like the Brotherhood, maybe a relative belonged? I'd better be careful, she thought, and if she brings it up again, I'll act as if I've forgotten all about it.

Mid-afternoon Emma stopped in the staffroom doorway when a roar of laughter broke out, and one woman shouted, 'You've got to be joking!'

Of the four women sitting at the table, three were laughing and one was beetroot red and looked as she was about to burst into tears. Paula was the youngest of the staff and Emma had often wondered if she was as innocent or ignorant as she made out. Could a twenty-two-year-old really be so utterly out of touch with the world in general and with current topics in particular?

The uproar had quietened down and Paula said plaintively, 'Well, how would I know what everyone was up to back then? I never heard of anything like that before.'

'What are you lot doing to Paula?' asked Emma and sat down. 'Are you tormenting her?'

'They are!' Paula, whose face was gradually returning to its normal pale, freckled state, turned to Emma. 'They're teasing me because I didn't believe what they were saying about some girl in that Mary Wesley book we've replaced. It just arrived and I was putting the stamp in it and Anne told me a bit about the story and that girl. And I said I didn't believe it.'

Anne laughed. 'We were discussing the selfish girl in

The Camomile Lawn, can't remember her name, oh wait, she's called Calypso – the one who goes to bed with practically everyone she meets in London during the second world war, promiscuous and on the hunt for a rich husband. And Paula said surely nobody did that back in the 1940's.' She grinned at Emma. 'Apparently Paula thinks back then everyone behaved like timid virgins and never had sex until they married.'

'Aha!' said Emma and smiled at Paula. 'Well, I think that girl was an extreme, even during the war when people apparently did things they'd never thought of doing before. But if you don't believe the fictional girl in the book, you should read the biography – Mary Wesley's I mean, the author of that book. It's an amazing story - it's called Wild Mary. And she *was* wild too, just like the character in that book.'

Chapter 6

After dinner Emma once again thought of the afternoon break and the conversation about *Wild Mary* and called her mother. 'Didn't you mention you were reading Wild Mary some time last year? I think you said you found it in that mega-sized book fair the high school has every year.'

'Yes, I did – I remember us talking about it. A very unusual woman. I don't normally like biographies – usually a lot of assumptions get included to make the story flow, and if it's just facts and photos they bore me.'

'Really?' said Emma, who had assumed her mother liked biographies. 'I thought you recommended Wild Mary?'

'Oh, I probably did – mostly because she was so outrageous and unusual. But generally speaking, I don't trust people who claim they remember the exact words they overheard when they were three years old. Autobiographies are the worst, full of sanitised reasons for past misdeeds, rewriting the script. And anyway, families all remember things differently – it's like we filter things through screens with holes of different dimensions. Like your father and I, we can't agree how anything happened or what anyone said.'

'Oh God, don't remind me,' said Emma and smiled to herself. 'I can still hear your voices saying "no, no, that's not what I said" and "no, that's not what happened". You were just totally unsuited as a couple despite what great parents you are. Different brain patterns or something.'

'Did he tell you he broke his arm?'

'*No!* When did this happen? I talked to him just a few days ago. He said his boat is booked solid right up to June, but he didn't mention his arm.'

'I think it happened a couple of weeks ago. He got them to put a fibreglass cast on his arm, so it doesn't matter if it gets wet. Typical of Martin, never stops for a moment, so he's out on that boat full of divers every day, probably getting water inside the cast – probably diving himself, too. I told him his arm will rot inside the cast if he doesn't take care.'

'I'll text him and ask how he's getting on. Did he tell you he's got a new girlfriend?'

'I think that's why he called.' Her mother chuckled. 'He doesn't call or email me very often, but it seems to be when he wants me to know he's not sitting around alone and miserable, that he's a desirable package still. This latest one's a dancer.'

'He didn't tell me that! Ballet? Nightclub?'

'Pole dancer,' said her mother with a chuckle and Emma laughed. 'No, don't laugh like that, it's true. You can ask him yourself if you don't believe me. It made me laugh, too.'

Emma tried to imagine what the pole dancer might look like and wondered if there was more to the pole dancing than her mother seemed to think.

'She's not a hooker, is she?' she asked, trying to sound casual. 'That would be a bit much to take in about one's dad.'

Her mother chuckled. 'I don't know, and it doesn't matter anyway. He said she's in her late thirties and very nice and a good cook, too. As opposed to me, I suppose.'

'But how does it he do it? All these women, not that they ever last very long. I don't get it. He's not that desirable is he?'

Somehow she had never considered how her father managed to have one girlfriend after another, or where he met them in the first place, but her mother's reply was prompt. 'He's a very sexy beast, your dad. Women have always flocked to him like bees around a honey pot. Middle age and scruffy stubble don't seem to put them off.' Now she laughed outright. 'When I left him for David several women friends of mine said I had to be mad to give him up for someone as "civilised" as

David – they meant he wasn't a sexy beast. I still remember your aunt Alison using the phrase. Turned out nearly all my friends had been attracted to your dad at some stage, not just the two or three, or maybe four, he took to bed.'

Emma was caught between laughing and feeling disgusted but pulled herself together and said, 'I didn't know all that stuff! And I still can't see him as a sexy beast, but I'll have to take your word for it. It's a weird thing to hear about your father, and what a thing to discover at my age – my dad's a sexy beast, wow.' She paused for a moment, and pictured her dad, thought that perhaps her mother was right. 'But why did you never mention this before, it's kind of fascinating. Did you think I'd be shocked or something?'

'I've no idea!' said her mother. 'I wasn't keeping it secret. It's probably just that it hasn't ever come up in conversation before.'

It wasn't until they finished their conversation that Emma realised that her mother didn't mention hearing from Catriona, so she texted a question and got a thumbs up emoticon in reply.

That night she woke up with a jerk from a nightmare about being underwater with her eyes wide open, holding her breath and not knowing what was up or what was down. The panicky feeling of being desperate for air and having lost her bearings made her gasp for air even when she woke up, as if she really had been holding her breath in her sleep. She read for a few moments and then her eyes shut by themselves, and she woke in the morning with the bedside light still on.

The text from Anne on the Sunday morning, was brief and to the point, 'Coffee at eleven at Bodley's?' and Emma replied yes and sat down to study for a couple of hours. It was only when she walked down to town that she remembered the dream in detail and thought how weird it was. She never took up diving despite her father's invitation to train her, and she didn't often go swimming, certainly not under water; probably never underwater. Isn't it odd, she thought, how things appear in dreams, and we have no idea where they came from, things we have no experience of.

Bodley's was full as usual on a Saturday morning, but Anne was at the best table in the window corner.

'How on earth did you manage this on a weekend morning?' asked Emma. 'I hope you didn't hover looking impatient until someone got intimidated and left? I know how ruthless you can be.'

'There was no need for ruthlessness, I'm just smart,' said Anne smugly. 'I got here about fifteen minutes ago and waited patiently just between the door and the window until the couple who had this table finished and then straight away I sat down and put my bag on the other chair. They did ask me to start with if I was waiting for a table, and I said I was just waiting for a friend out of the wind. And I didn't stare at them, so you can take that suspicious look off your face. I love this table and we don't often get it, hardly ever. So, now you'll have to order for me – if we both go someone will nick our table.'

When Emma was paying for their order she noticed the letter she had picked up from the mailbox in the lobby when she got home the previous night, which she had stuffed in her bag when she got her keys out and then forgotten about. Now she slid her finger under the flap as she walked back to their table.

'Oh damn - what a big increase!' She sat down holding the letter up in the air and looked dismayed at Anne. 'The second anniversary of my lease is coming up this winter – I'd forgotten it was due for a rent review.'

Anne took it out of her hand and glanced at it. 'Mm – that's quite a lot, particularly for a two-year lease. Can you afford it?'

'It wasn't cheap to start with, but I felt I could manage if I was careful with other spending. It's such a lovely flat and nearly brand new, and I loved the idea of having a balcony. But an additional fifteen percent! Oh, well, I'll just have to be even more careful.'

She looked at the letter again. 'I've got to agree by the thirty-first of May and the increase takes effect on the first of July.'

'But listen,' said Anne when their order had been delivered. 'The way Cora asked all those questions about the letter you found, wasn't that weird? Did you understand where she was coming from?'

Emma took a sip of coffee and made a quick decision about how much she was prepared to tell Anne. After the second encounter with Cora, she felt a need to keep everything to herself, even when talking to someone like Anne, whom she trusted, but she would reveal the harmless details.

'She did it again, you know,' she said. 'Yesterday morning when we met in the restroom. She came in while I was washing my hands and straight away started talking about it again – asked if I could bring the letter in for her to look at.'

'She's a bit random at times,' said Anne. 'Sometimes I can't work out what goes on in her head. What did she ask yesterday?'

'She wanted to know the names of who wrote it and who to, and then she asked me to bring the letter in, so I told her I threw it in the bin. I mean it was over thirty years old. Did she think I'd keep it?'

Anne looked thoughtful and Emma took a bite of her almond croissant, mentally making a decision to only have coffee next time and stop spending money on expensive pastries in cafes.

'Listen,' said Anne after a moment. 'You might not know this, but Cora's brother works for the City Council – he's the assistant to the CEO.'

She paused and Emma looked expectantly at her, wondering where this was going. 'And?'

'Well, this might be a bit far-fetched, but it kind of fits. Some years ago, when the mobs stormed the Capitol building in Washington, Cora said she and her brother had had a terrible fight about it and they weren't on speaking terms any longer. He's one of those Voices for Freedom people, that lot who turn up whenever anyone protests against anything. So, the other morning I wondered if that name - the Brotherhood - might be something she knows he's involved with, because it seemed to ring a bell. You didn't see her face, but she reacted very strongly as soon as you said it.'

'Could be, I suppose,' said Emma, doing her best to sound slightly sceptical, though her brain was buzzing. 'We did mention that group. Is her brother a lot younger than she is? That tall, gangly guy who came along with the mayor and all the top people when we opened the extension last year. I think she said he was there.'

'That's him, built like a beanstalk and slightly stooped – I'd forgotten he was there that day. But you must have noticed him hanging around looking at you when he comes in. So, what *did* the letter say about the Brotherhood? Anything interesting?'

'What *are* you talking about?' Emma stared disbelieving at Anne. 'He doesn't hang around, he hardly ever comes in and when he does he's on inside for five minutes.'

'About once a month, I think,' said Anne calmly.

'He borrows back numbers of those specialist monthly magazines about IT and technical things, and then he returns them a week later, he's been doing it forever. But since you've been here he tends to lurk – he kind of pretends he's looking at something, but he keeps a close eye on the checkout desk until the other person there is busy and then he swoops in, so he can talk to you.'

'I'm not interested, so it doesn't matter,' said Emma. 'I'm not attracted to men who look like a fillet of fish. I go more for the solid, broad type of man, the kind you can lean on in a storm.'

'Ok, but don't be surprised if he asks you out - if he can get up the courage. He probably already knows you're single, he can find out anything he likes from Cora.'

'I thought you said they weren't on speaking terms. Have they patched it up?'

'God yes, ages ago. He's her baby brother, and she loves him. So, tell me, did you go home and get the letter out of the rubbish, so you could tell Cora those names?'

No more of this, thought Emma, it's getting tricky. 'No, of course I didn't! Let Cora fret about it, I don't really care. There was nothing in that letter of any interest – a thirty-year-old letter isn't of any real historical value, and it was just a lot of stuff about family and what they were reading.'

Make it seem dull, she thought, and extinguish this little flame of gossip right now. 'But listen to this – you know I told you my dad likes to brag every time he has a new girlfriend, he tells me or mum. It's like he needs to demonstrate he's still got it. It's kind of sweet and he's had a few girlfriends since they split up, but they never seem to last. I bet you can't guess what the latest one does for a living.'

Walking back up the hill, Emma considered the implications of Anne's comment about Cora's brother and wondered if perhaps Cora knew her brother was connected to the Brotherhood, because that would explain her reaction to the name and why she wanted the details, but maybe that was one coincidence to many and because her mind was full of it she saw connections everywhere. She wished she hadn't mentioned the name Miller or the Brotherhood, but maybe nobody else would link the two things.

Was that chance or intention, wondered Emma on Monday morning in the staff room when Anne initiated a discussion about the local body elections in October. She never knew with Anne, who had a very strategic mind and enjoyed a good hard debate, sometimes with slightly evil intent, like the time she'd overheard Paula mention her uncle being in trouble over a pub fight, and Anne brought up how she'd read a piece in the paper about a brawl outside a pub as if by chance, and poor Paula got so embarrassed.

'I know I'm way ahead of myself,' Anne said now, 'but I'm intrigued by the amount of talk about the local elections so early this time. I'm sure it wasn't always like this, the election's nearly half a year away. All these keen people announcing they want to be the next mayor and acting like they're important already.'

'It's probably because the mayors of three major cities have said they're retiring all at the same time,' said Cora and reached for the biscuits. 'It's a massive change and all the candidates are taking the opportunity to start a bit of self-promotion in advance. Those two candidates in Christchurch came right out of the blue and they never stood for anything before, not even the school board. It's quite unusual. And you're right, they've started way ahead of when that kind of posturing normally starts.'

'And one complete unknown in Auckland,' said Paula, who had never before voiced an opinion on anything political, and who rarely seemed to keep up with current affairs. 'That rich guy with the gorgeous wife. He's popping up in video clips on social media. He sounds like he'd be good – just like he says, he's a new voice and he's got common sense. And his wife wears beautiful clothes that look as if they cost thousands. I always check her out.'

Anne glanced sideways at Emma, raised an eyebrow and said, 'I know who you mean, and the wife is *very* expensive looking. He might be a good potential mayor, decisive and clear, and he's got a whole list of issues he wants to tackle – that city needs to sort itself out before it becomes a real mess.'

'You mean what's-his-name Miller,' said Cora and took another biscuit. 'From what I've heard he's got some good qualities. And you're right, Paula – his wife's lovely. God knows how she's managed to stay so slim after three children.'

Emma took no part in the brief discussion that followed, careful to keep out of anything that included the name Miller, but she paid special attention to everything Cora said and how she said it. Anything related to Gerald Miller was interesting, as was Cora's possible connection to the Brotherhood, even if it was at one remove.

That evening Emma sat down with a pad and a calculator and carefully worked through her fixed expenses. She went through her credit card and bank account and noted down spending she would probably have overlooked otherwise. She tried to imagine the unexpected emergencies that might crop up. Car disasters, she thought, tapping her front teeth with the pencil, some kind of major repair, perhaps five or six hundred or even a thousand dollars' worth. How would I cope with that? But the only thing she could do was start setting aside a set amount each payday into a second savings account to accumulate into a reserve fund for emergencies. In the back of her mind, she admitted that giving in to temptation to take this particular apartment might have been a mistake. It was only as she walked to work the next day that she realised that the car itself could be her reserve, and if all else failed she could sell it and buy a cheaper car. The thought cheered her but from a long-term angle it made no sense. Sooner or later a cheaper and older car would need the kind of expensive repairs that she might not be able to afford anyway. A future without a car was hard to contemplate, but she could do it if she had to. With the issue unresolved she arrived at work, slightly cheered by the knowledge that if she was going to give up the lease, she had a bit of time to work out what to do, and in the meantime she wouldn't discuss it with anyone. She had known from the start that moving to the South Island made visiting her mother far more expensive than staying where she was, but at the time she had a strong urge to start with a clean slate somewhere far away, and now those visits might be very far apart.

The next morning Catriona texted and said, 'Want to see something funny? Get on Skype!'

And there were the twins in side-by-side highchairs eating porridge with their hands. 'What do you think?' said Catriona. 'Let me do a sweep so you can see it all.' She slowly turned her phone to take in the mess on the kitchen floor and a grinning Duncan leaning against the fridge with the mop and bucket ready for the clean-up.

'We're thinking of getting a dog,' he said. 'You know, to make the mopping operation quicker - once the dog's gobbled up the lumps it won't take many minutes. Did you notice their hair?'

The phone swung back to the twins again and Emma laughed. Both darkhaired twins had smeared porridge into their hair, their faces were covered and one of them was squeezing porridge in his fist and watching it come out between his fingers.

'What a lovely mess! You should get a dog like Duncan said. Think about it, first the dog cleans the floor then you put the boys on the floor, and he licks them too – perfect solution.'

Catriona laughed. 'I never appreciated how good it was a few months ago when they were entirely breast-fed. I'd sit there with one of them on a cushion on my lap, sometimes both at the same time, and read. I propped my Kindle against the baby and re-read the classics. I remember being halfway through Pride and Prejudice when Rowan pooped in the middle of a very emotional scene, and I continued despite the smell till I reached the end of the chapter.'

While she was reading the news online over breakfast, as she did every day, Emma suddenly stopped and scrolled up to take a second look at something that she had nearly passed over. The phrase 'the necessity to introduce more tailored immigration' appeared as a quote from a speech by the prime minister. She looked up from the screen and wondered if there was a connection or if she was being paranoid. Just a couple of days ago, she had read an article about Gerald Miller, where he was quoted as using that exact wording when he commented on immigration policy, and the word necessity had stuck in her mind.

That article was about an interview over lunch with two women journalists, who described him as charming, unassuming and frank. She had looked at the photo of Miller sitting at an outside table at the

Viaduct Basin with glittering water behind him and tried to imagine the various implications of tailored immigration. It was obviously reflected in the current policies, to favour highly skilled people or those with skills in short supply in New Zealand as had always been the case. But when she considered that Miller might be a white supremacist and a racist and, then it might mean something else, something worse. He had a given coy and slightly evasive reply when the interviewer asked if he was aiming for central government based on how many of his opinions related to government policies.

Speculating further she imagined how it might lead to gradually decreasing the number of coloured immigrants and achieving a mostly white pool of newcomers. Stealth racism, she thought, a kind of racial purification by starting small and tweaking the percentages over time. Exactly the kind of regulation someone who believed in the supremacy of the white race would want to implement, but only vaguely phrased, open to interpretation. The article concluded with a quote from Miller that he believed women added a dimension currently lacking in politics and on boards of various kinds, that women balanced the debates by their "humanity" and she shook her head at the memory of that ludicrous expression. Vote grabbing, she said out loud. Trying to appeal to everyone. Two women journalists and a handsome and charming man; she wondered who paid for the lunch.

There had been a lack of journalistic digging-in in that article; no probing questions, no challenges. Maybe she was being too critical because she had recently tried to find out if the Brotherhood group still existed, and she was suspicious of Miller. Surely journalists were used to see through simple ploys like charm and a free lunch and wouldn't be so easily swayed into reporting everything at face value. And she had to admit that Miller was very good looking, and he couldn't help that or the fact that women obviously found him charming. He was a master of self-presentation and had great general appeal.

She got up to make another piece to toast and tried to put her finger on what made him such an effective campaigner, apart from his looks. Probably that middle-of-the-road aura he radiated of having something for everyone, always described as friendly and modest, no extremism detectable in his opinions. He had built an image of a sensible and caring man with genuinely good intentions, but when she read his quoted words with the ideas in his grandfather's letter in the back of her mind, the picture looked different.

She admitted to herself that she was prejudiced and leaping to conclusions and decided to make another attempt to find out if the Brotherhood group mentioned in the letter by Miller senior still existed, because the results so far were disappointing. There was nothing of the kind she was looking for, nothing to link the word brotherhood to anything like a group of that kind in New Zealand. The word had been used extensively all over the world for a wide variety of things for decades; motorbike gangs, bands, anime films, TV series and even a barber shop somewhere, and it had been used by protest movements in Egypt and other countries.

She got ready for work feeling discouraged and wondering if she was becoming obsessed and slightly paranoid. Because what was she actually doing? She was trying to extrapolate the mention of a group in a letter from more than thirty years ago into today's political world but finding no strong connections. Feeling disappointed was ridiculous, she told herself, she should be relieved and channel her energies in other directions, but now that the suspicion had taken root in her mind, she knew it would not be easily dislodged. And as she had sometimes done lately, she wondered if she was letting thoughts and ideas take over her mental world because she spent so much time alone, having nobody to interact with face to face after work or most weekends. She must make an effort, create a circle of friends, join something or take up offers from Anne to join her and her friends more often.

On Fridays Emma and Anne often went out after work for a pre-dinner drink, a habit that had slowly developed over the last year. Tonight, Emma looked across the table at her friend's slightly worried face and said, 'Is something wrong? Was that phone call just as we left bad news?'

Anne hesitated before she picked up her glass of chardonnay then said, 'I'm worried about Chris – he says he's gay.' She made a face and added quickly, 'I don't mind him being gay, if he really *is* gay, but he seems too young to know *what* he is, don't you think? He's only twelve. He called to say he's told his classmates he's gay but he's still on the rugby team – that's the team that plays seven-aside rugby in the lunchbreak at school. He thought I'd be pleased that he's still popular with his mates.'

'I think that's sweet,' said Emma and smiled. 'And how lucky you are that he tells you things like that – a lot of kids probably wouldn't. My friend Fletcher was always very popular at high school too because he's very physical and athletic, and everyone wanted him on their team. He's been known to be gay since year nine. It didn't seem to make any difference to anything.'

'So, he was what - thirteen when he came out? Has he ever told you how young he was when he first thought he was gay?'

'I've no idea, I don't think we've ever talked about it. I know the girls still thought he was very sexy - they probably still do. Don't worry about Chris, just let him do his thing and see what happens. But I must say that to me twelve seems plenty old enough to know who you fancy. I knew the kind of man I liked by the age of twelve or thirteen, had no doubts at all and I've never changed my mind.'

On the way home she thought of Fletcher, so comfortable in his own skin, and so self-assured. Most women who met him probably never thought of the word "gay" in connection with him. And possibly most men didn't either, as he had never displayed any of the stereotypical mannerisms that some people associated with gay men. And then a thought struck her, and she laughed at herself, because how would she know if some men she met were gay if they were like Fletcher? There'd be nothing to make her think they were. How funny, she thought, that this had never occurred to her before.

Chapter 8

Emma was sitting up in bed with a cup of tea after waking up far too early, when an email from Nadine; a girl she had not had any contact with since their student days, arrived on her phone. They had been quite close friends at university, but after an incident that never got properly resolved they drifted apart. It's a strange time of the day to write emails, thought Emma, but perhaps no stranger than me sitting here at this hour reading one.

She postponed replying until she had given herself time to process what Nadine had written, to really absorb it and then respond in a balanced and unemotional way. She and Nadine hadn't met or had any contact since they completed their studies, and in the year before that, they had become distanced by an event that Emma still regretted. She had tried to warn Nadine about a boy she had just started dating, a boy who was known to have been physically rough with girls more than once, and Nadine hadn't taken it well.

It was probably her own fault that it ended with an estrangement between them, thought Emma now, as she looked back at the incident. She had been nervous about broaching the subject, not diplomatic enough and the result was little or no direct contact in their last year. After her shower Emma read the email again, still uncertain about how to respond.

Hi Emma, Catriona gave me your email address and phone number, as the ones I had from years ago had changed. I live in Cambridge these days, and I am on a three-week trip around the South Island to see the sights, visit relatives and hopefully catch up with some old friends. I called Catriona from the ferry when I remembered I had heard that you live down here, so it's short notice. I'm not sure exactly how long I'll spend at each stop, but I'm heading south along the east coast, staying with an aunt in Kaikoura tonight and maybe tomorrow. I know we haven't been in touch for a long time, and I was very sorry to hear about the tragedies in your life (from Catriona). Had I known about the accident at the time, I would have got in touch, and now it's very late in the piece, but I want to extend my sympathy and love, hoping it will count for something. Kind regards and a hug, Nadine.

. . .

After some thought while she had breakfast Emma replied.

Hi Nadine, It's nice to hear from you and thank you for your message. Kind thoughts count even now, of course — just like grief, sympathy has no use-by date. If it suits your schedule to spend a night here you're welcome to stay at my place. I don't have a guest room, but the fold-out sofa is very comfortable, and it wouldn't be a problem. Cheers, Emma.

That will do, thought Emma when she had read through it again. It's friendly enough and offering her the chance to spend the night means she knows I don't harbour any silly old resentments. The fact that she called me an interfering bitch at the time, is neither here nor there; I might have done the same if someone had tried to warn me about a new love.

Four days later Nadine texted to say she had spent more time than planned in Kaikoura and Canterbury, so in order to fit her vague schedule of family visits, she could not spend a night with Emma but would love to have lunch, if Emma told her what time and where would suit her the following day.

'If you don't mind I'll skip my lunch break today and take a longer break tomorrow,' said Emma to Cora that morning. 'I'm having lunch with an old friend I haven't seen for years – a fellow librarian. Would that be OK with you?'

'Fine with me,' said Cora. 'You're always so punctual – not like some of the others who are always late in the mornings.'

Waiting outside the French Bistro by the park the next day, Emma was pleased the day was sunny and then laughed at herself for being parochial. But there's nothing wrong with wanting your town to look nice when someone's coming to visit, she thought, it's a bit like making sure your house is tidy when you expect visitors; it's about making a good impression.

'Good lord!' said Nadine and laughed when she arrived a few minutes later and hugged Emma. 'How on earth do you do it? You look the same as you did last time I saw you – must be ten years ago.'

'It's lovely to see you! I'm glad you got in touch,' said Emma, after a quick decision to not respond to the comment about her appearance and led the way inside. 'I've booked a table to make sure we get a good one where people don't walk past behind us all the time to get in and out. This place is so oblong, like a long corridor, but the menu is fantastic.'

When they were seated opposite each other, she thought how lucky it was that Nadine had come straight up to her with that hug, or she might not have recognised her, because the tall slim girl from a decade ago was no longer recognisable, and only the startling blue-green eyes and the long-fingered hands remained unchanged.

'Listen, there's something I need to say first up,' Emma said, hoping she wasn't going to ruin their lunch, but it was important to clear up this unresolved issue from the past. 'I was standing outside thinking about that time in our last year when I told you about what's-his-name - James - and you got so upset. I'm sorry I was such a klutz! I should have been more diplomatic, but I was nervous about bringing it up at all, so I made a real mess of it.'

Nadine looked at her as if in disbelief, slowly moving her head from side to side. 'You've been worried about *that*? You've got to be kidding! *You* didn't make a mess of it, I did. I was rude and aggressive when you tried to warn me, and it took a while before I admitted to myself that I had over-reacted. Defensiveness, I think. I didn't want to admit I'd made a mistake – which I was beginning to suspect myself even at that stage. And then when I found out that he was really like that, well, it was kind of too late to say anything, and we had already drifted apart, hadn't we?'

Emma stretched here neck to look over at the booth behind Nadine to make sure nobody was sitting there before she asked something personal. 'I knew you split up with him a while later, friends told me about it and I've always wondered if he hurt you too, I mean physically – if that's why you broke up with him?'

'No, he didn't hurt me, but he had a terrible, explosive temper, and then my brother told me that he had punched a girl when he was at high school and given her a black eye. So, I broke up with him to avoid getting into trouble. That temper was a real turn-off.'

Their lunch turned into an hour of reminiscing about their time as students and catching up on news about old friends, and when the waiter had taken their lunch plates away and they had ordered coffee, Nadine said, 'This is such fun! I'm so glad you had time to see me. I met up with Jerry in Nelson, remember him, the shy one with the peculiar ears? We had lunch, but it didn't go well.' She frowned. 'I don't think I'll ever get in touch with him again – not even on social media. He's turned into something I never thought I'd see, not from him. He was such a nice, quiet guy at college, seemed so … normal.'

'What's happened to him? Drugs or something?'

'No, but he's become a radical in every respect you can imagine – far-right redneck aggressiveness. He spent the whole lunch expounding his opinions about gays, liberals and other sickos as he called them, and he made some toxic racist comments – totally overlooked the fact that I'm half Maori, which he's obviously aware of. And listen to this, some of the things he said made me worry he's delusional – or maybe on drugs, as you said.' Nadine shook her head as if she still found it hard to believe. '*Change is coming*, he kept saying in a significant voice like it was a mantra or something, change is coming. I think he said it half a dozen times like it was a meaningful message I should talk note of. He tried to grill me on which candidates I'll vote for in the elections next spring! I told him I don't even know who they are yet – nobody does, it's far too early. *And* he believes in multiple conspiracy theories. I think we can safely say he's disappearing fast down that nasty rabbit hole.'

Emma waited while their coffee was delivered and said, 'I've had a very interesting time lately with something a bit similar but based in the past. Have you read about that guy Miller in Auckland, the rich guy who's already announced he's standing for mayor of Auckland?'

'Of course,' said Nadine and grinned. 'You'd have to live under a rock to avoid reading about him. He's got a huge talent for self-promotion, and he's also great looking and seems like a nice guy. What about him? Something from the past, some youthful act of silliness or something worse?'

Emma told her the story about finding the old letter in the maths book, then got her phone out. 'It was the name connection that made me curious,' she said. 'And the more I researched it the more intriguing it became. I've got photos on my phone of the whole letter and the envelope – both sides. Here, see for yourself.'

She passed her phone to Nadine with the image folder open and noticed a waiter heading to their corner with a plate in his hand and felt uneasy. She had got carried away, and now there was obviously someone in the booth behind Nadine who could have heard the whole conversation. Nadine looked up from Emma's phone and was about to comment on what she had read, but Emma held a finger to her lips, pointed to the booth behind her and shook her head. Taking her phone out of Nadine's hand, she quickly typed a text message and without sending it just handed her phone back across the table. *Don't comment, there's someone behind you, let's talk about this outside. Don't let him see your face. I'll pay and meet you outside.*

'God, you're really worried about this for some reason,' said Nadine five minutes later as they walked through the park. 'Why? Talking about the letter doesn't seem dangerous, and we're hundreds of miles away from Auckland.'

'I do feel worried about it,' said Emma and turned to look directly at Nadine to make sure she would see she was serious. 'I'd rather people didn't know I was delving into this like some kind of research project. Imagine how awful it would be if it got out and I was wrong. It would be defamation it could cause all kinds of trouble, start a media storm, start rumours that can't be stopped and damage Miller's prospects, because I don't even know if that group still exists. But there's no doubt the man, who wrote the letter, is the grandfather of the current Miller. And I presume you noticed the discrepancy about the names on the envelope and in the letter?'

'Oh, yes, very odd! You've got me really intrigued now - let's sit down on that seat over there. I'd like to hear a bit more before you have to go back to work, if you don't mind telling me. And I'd love to look at those photos again, this is like a mystery novel.'

Emma outlined her ideas about what she had found and how things linked into a credible whole, and Nadine asked question after question until there was no time left, and no more to be gained by discussing it further.

'Riveting!' said Nadine when they parted. 'That's the most interesting lunch I've had in my whole life and thanks for sharing all that stuff. I promise not to tell anyone about it unless you give me the all-clear. We must keep in touch!'

Chapter 9

On the following Monday morning, after a weekend of intensive work completing a challenging physics assignment, Emma arrived at work to find Cora and a man she didn't recognise waiting for her. They were standing just in front of the desk, and as soon as Emma came towards them, Cora said, 'Emma, this is Mr McLean from the City Council's HR office – he's here to see you.' Without waiting for a reply, she turned to the man and said, 'Use my office, I've got plenty of things I can do out here.'

As soon as they were in Cora's office, McLean handed Emma a sealed envelope while they were still standing and said rather abruptly, 'I'm sorry about this, but this is an official notice of redundancy. Over the last several months the library has overspent its budget without anyone at the council noticing by quite how much, and to remedy the situation we have to make one staff member redundant. And you're the most recently hired, so it has to be you, I'm afraid.'

For a moment Emma's mind refused to take it in; to walk in the door for another routine day at work and be taken aside like this and told she was losing her job was devastating. She stood silent for a few moments with the envelope in her hand until she found her voice and said, 'Why me? Being hired last isn't a good reason is it? I'm a qualified librarian, one of only two here. Is that of no value?'

'It wasn't my decision,' said McLean quickly, embarrassed and avoiding meeting her eyes. 'It seems they used that old principle of "last hired, first fired" — it doesn't seem reasonable when you're fully trained, I must admit. As you say, it's only Mrs Gordon and you who are fully qualified. But there's nothing I can do about it. You could lodge a formal complaint directly with the HR manager, but as it stands now, your last day will be two weeks from last Friday, seeing you're paid fortnightly.' Then he smiled, as if he had just thought of something good, and added, 'And we'll pay out your accumulated holiday entitlement, of course.'

'If I leave right now, do I still get paid for the notice period, I mean the fortnight that has just begun today?'

McLean looked uncomfortable and said, again without meeting her eyes, 'I don't know - I'll have to contact my manager. Could you wait here please?'

Emma's head was full of conflicting thoughts, but one stood out as urgent. As McLean moved towards the door she said quickly, 'And if I can leave directly, I want an email sent to me right now stating that I will still both get this fortnight's pay and my accumulated leave money.'

He was only gone for a couple of minutes and came back into the room with a satisfied smile, as if he had personally achieved something good. He's really embarrassed at having been sent on this errand, thought Emma, and now he feels he has done something for me – thank God, I don't have his job. And how can they send a clerical person or whatever he is to do this? Shouldn't the HR manager have done it?

'Yes to all your questions,' he said and closed the door behind him again. 'The email will come within minutes, directly from my manager.' He hesitated for a moment before he added, 'And just so you know, I checked your employment agreement before I came over and it's the standard City Council version, so there's no redundance pay-out and your copy of it contains details about the procedure for lodging a complaint in case that's what you want to do.'

'If due process has been followed, what could I complain about?' asked Emma, who already knew a reason, but she wanted to hear what he would say.

'You could use the fact that apart from Mrs Gordon you're the only fully qualified librarian here since Ms Dalgety retired last year. It might work but it will take time, and you would probably need legal advice to back you up.' He hesitated for a moment. 'But the "last hired, first fired" thing's been used before at the Council, so it might have set some kind of precedent. I don't really know.'

Emma thought this might be his first sacking, or perhaps he felt he was being forced to act on a principle he didn't agree with. The way he talked about process for deciding who should leave seemed to indicate he didn't think it was right.

When Emma's phone pinged with an email alert she got it out of her bag and read the message from the HR manager, put the phone back in her bag and said, 'I'll stay until we have morning tea and then pick up my things and leave. Please see to it that I get a proper reference – one that states I was made redundant and the reason for it, so it doesn't look as if I was sacked for some misdemeanour.' And then another thought popped into her head, and she added, 'Do you think you could give me the over-spend figures for the year to date – compared to the budget?'

McLean stared at her for a few moments before he shook his head. 'I've no idea how to do that or what the rules are. I think a written request to the finance department would be the only way – it's not something for HR to decide, I wouldn't think.'

The next hour was made unnecessarily uncomfortable by Cora, who seemed unable to decide if she should acknowledge what had just taken place or just ignore it. She was keeping herself busy and initiated no conversation with Emma but kept glancing at her, so until their pre-opening coffee time, Emma did what she would have done on any other working day, while worried thoughts circled like sharks in her head.

Anne came across from the children's section, looking worried and confused, and spoke in a low voice as they walked together towards the staff room. 'Are you in some sort of trouble? That guy's from the HR department, isn't he? I saw him there when I went in to pick up a form for my friend's daughter a few months ago.'

'Wait a few minutes,' said Emma and swallowed hard. 'I'll tell everyone at the same time.' She didn't know if she would be able to hold her composure together if she had to repeat the information more than once, and she refused to show how distressed she was. Every second since she first heard McLean say the word "redundant" she had felt she was under threat, that what she had thought of a secure and contented life was rocking on its foundations. But for now, she must steel herself, do what had to be done with as much dignity as possible and then leave.

Walking home felt like skipping school, as if she was doing something furtive, something others would disapprove of. At midmorning on a weekday, the sidewalks were noticeably emptier, though the traffic was a busy as ever. In her mind she started making a list of what she must do now that she was officially unemployed. Searching the Internet for job vacancies was the first thing but applying for anything would have to wait until she had her reference. Being able to demonstrate in a job application that she had been made redundant was important to avoid anyone suspecting she had been sacked or had agreed to resign.

Emma knew resignations didn't always mean what the seemed to mean. She had heard enough stories about employees who had avoided being sacked for a serious offence by agreeing to resign immediately and voluntarily in exchange for a sum of money. The first time she had heard about this, Catriona had told her that part of a deal like that is always that neither party reveal it was not a genuine resignation.

'The evil ways of the world, but not insurmountable,' Catriona had said, when Emma asked how someone would know a job searcher was not a risk if they employed them.

'They might hire someone who's going to cause trouble,' Emma had said indignantly. 'It's like rewarding someone who's done something bad instead of just sacking them.'

'Oh no, not completely,' Catriona had said calmly. 'A person like that won't get a reference like most would – no mention of good qualities etc. They'll usually just get a statement of employment with the role they held and the start and finish dates, nothing else. Potential employers know how to interpret that, so if they're smart they'll ask questions informally to find out what's behind it.'

'I still don't see what good it is,' Emma had said at the time. 'Sacking them would be cheaper, wouldn't it?'

Catriona smiled at Emma's naiveté. 'Think of it like this – a sacked employee might lay a formal complaint about unfair dismissal, threaten to take them to the employment court, drag it out endlessly. And if the misdeed isn't an instant sacking offence, then continuing having the person in the workplace working out a notice period is risky. They might cause trouble in various ways before they leave, including sabotage, often IT sabotage. Big companies, banks and law firms particularly, don't want those kinds of things becoming public – especially if it involves theft or fraud. It would be detrimental to their reputation, destroy the trust of their customers and so on. And paying people out always involves signed agreements that both sides will keep up the pretence the person left voluntarily. And neither side can reveal there was a payment or how much it was.'

Now Emma covered the last stretch up the hill while mentally scrolling through employment options; the first one was the university library, followed by the court, then the high schools and last and least desirable, looking further afield to smaller town which would involve a move.

Two hours later she had Googled all the potential workplaces on her mental list, checked their websites for "job opportunities" and found none. Online employment websites had nothing closer than Wellington, which would mean the expense of moving back to the North Island if she got the job, with all the accompanying hassles of finding somewhere to live that she could afford. She spent half the afternoon chasing head librarians and headmasters by phone and managed to connect with all but two; there were no known future vacancies and no staff taking parental leave. At four her phone pinged with a message from Fletcher: *Lunch tomorrow? I'll be in town for a few hours.*

They arranged to meet at the Little Coffee House as usual and Emma finally gave in to the naggin worry about her rent increase and opened the spreadsheet she had compiled to study it more closely. She went through it over and over, but the result was still the same. If she couldn't get a job at the same rate of pay or better than she had at the library she could not risk keeping the apartment. She must get a well-paid job that started before the end of May which was the date by which she must confirm or refuse the rent increase. There was no way she would risk accepting the increase, even though it didn't take effect until July. What if she couldn't get a job that paid well enough? She would be forced to break the rent contract and might get involved in legal issues that required expensive lawyers.

That night sleep was impossible and by morning she felt more tired than she had when she went to bed.

But while tossing and turning and trying to work something out, one clear thought had crystallized in her mind. She would start looking for a cheaper flat right away and decline the rent increase at the same time. Be proactive and make sure things don't go badly wrong, she told herself as she looked at herself in the bathroom mirror while drying her hair. Having spent two years in a perfect, modern flat didn't mean she couldn't live in something smaller, maybe a studio apartment or even a bedsit. Finding something might be difficult, as it always was once the academic year had started and reasonably priced accommodation became very hard to find, but if she started now, surely she would find something before she had to leave her present flat at the end of June.

Chapter 10

Fletcher was waiting when Emma arrived at the Little Coffee House and as usual he noticed immediately that something was wrong. Holding her away from himself after pulling her into a hug, he studied her face for a moment and said, 'What's happened? Something's not right – anything I can help with?'

'Nothing's wrong, I'm just tired after a night of practically no sleep,' said Emma and smiled, reluctant to let their lunch date be ruined by depressing news. 'Let's go inside out of this wind. And I want to hear every single last detail about the famous wedding.'

He might not have believed her, but it was also very like Fletcher to say nothing more about it. The found a table and ordered before conversation resumed.

'I suppose you saw all the online publicity - yes? So, let's say the wedding itself was a success, as was the before-party and the after-party. We got our huge bonus, and the damage was limited to one expensive leather armchair, a dozen or so glasses and a shattered tibia.'

'A shattered what?' asked Emma, who thought she must have misheard what he said. 'It sounded like you said tibia.'

'I did say tibia, as in the bone in the lower leg.' Fletcher grinned at her face and got his phone out. 'This is a picture of the event that caused it. These clowns were up on the roof of the cabana by the outdoor pool at some ungodly time of the morning – three of them, all males of course, with drinks in their hands, yahooing and carrying on. Night security called me, and I was just coming along to help talk them down, when one of them shouted 'we'll come down right away if you take a photo of us first'. So, trying to avoid some kind of stand-off I got my phone out to take a photo of them, but they started clowning around, striking poses and one fell onto the tiled surround inside the pool fence and landed *very* badly on his leg. I swear I heard the crack as that bone snapped.'

'Didn't you say they were on the cabana roof? Isn't the cabana inside the fence? How did they get in there at that time of the night?'

Fletcher moved his phone to one side so the waiter could put their cutlery down and said, 'It is, but they got on the roof via the stone wall behind the cabana, balanced along the top of a seven-foot wall - drunk as skunks and with glasses in their hands. God knows how!'

Emma noticed the expression on the waiter's face and thought this might be the most exciting comment he had overheard that week. Fletcher passed the phone across and watched her face as she flicked through the pictures.

'It looks like a sequence of shots from a film,' she said and went through them again. 'But at least you've got it documented that they were on that roof. And the shot of the guy falling through the air. How did you get that? The way his glass is flying along upright beside him - marvellous!'

'Unintended.' Fletcher took the phone back and laughed. 'I must have just kept my finger on the button and the camera went into burst-mode and took a photo or two every second until I took my finger off. And did you notice I got a shot in at the beginning that shows the sign on the pool gate – closed, meaning locked, at nine every night.'

The rest of the lunch was spent discussing the famous and not quite famous guests at the wedding and how lovely the ceremony had been, performed in the so-called winter garden, which looked like a giant glasshouse full of tropical plants. 'But tell me,' said Emma and spread plum sauce on a piece of corn fritter. 'What happened to the expensive leather armchair? Another drunk?'

'Just a woman who seemed to be intent on making

sure she was always the centre of attention. I can't tell you her name, but she is middling famous in the US TV industry, friend of the bride's. She created little scenarios all over the place to get people to stop talking and watch her. The staff told me story after story about her later. The chair was ruined when she got up on it in a dress so short you could see the under-curve of her bum under the hem and danced on it in four-inch stiletto heels. About thirty puncture marks on the seat.' He laughed again. 'It came to an undignified end when one heel went so far through the leather that it got stuck. She fell forward over the back of the chair and showed her bum and her thong to the world – and the heel broke.'

But suddenly Fletcher stopped the reminiscing and put his knife and fork down. 'Now let's stop this for a moment. I *know* something's wrong, Emma. Tell me!'

'It's still so new - and raw, I suppose you'd call it. I haven't told anyone yet because it only happened yesterday and ...'

'And what? Is it too personal to talk about?' Fletcher was looking worried, perhaps thinking he had pushed too hard and embarrassed her. Emma knew she must tell him now, to avoid him feeling bad, and he might also have useful advice, but it felt as if she hadn't processed things properly and getting emotional in public was unthinkable.

'I was sacked yesterday morning when I arrived at

work.' She put it bluntly, not sure what the next step was. Should she go into detail or just skate over it?

Fletcher's eyebrows pulled together, and he looked hard at her. 'You, sacked? I don't believe it. Why? What had you done?'

'Sorry,' said Emma, realising she had given him the wrong impression. 'I used the wrong word — I was made redundant, but it felt like I was sacked. Apparently the library budget's been overspent for some time and nobody at the council had realised and now the must reign it in, so I'm the one who's got to go. The guy who came to give me the formal letter said, "last hired, first fired". Apparently that's a policy at the council, but I haven't checked my employment contract yet to see if it's mentioned.'

'He said what?!' Fletcher was outraged and his voice rose slightly. 'I never heard anything to ridiculous - that's totally unacceptable in today's world. And didn't you say when you moved here that you were replacing a qualified librarian?'

'I was hired because one was about to retire, and that would have left just one qualified person, the head librarian. And now Cora *will* be the only one. My training doesn't seem to come into it.'

'I'll ask a few questions about this,' said Fletcher, scowling ferociously. 'We've got a really good lawyer for the lodge, and I sometimes ask her for advice when we have problems with staff.'

Emma finished her corn fritter and silently debated

with herself if she should tell him about the rent rise as well, because the feeling of relief at having shared yesterday's shock had somehow made her feel a bit better. 'And at the same time, I've got a problem with my flat – the rent review is due, and the increase is quite steep, so unless I get a job before…' her voice broke, and she knew she was close to tears.

Fletcher got to his feet. 'Come on - let's go back to your flat. This isn't the right place,' he said. 'I want to hear more about this. We'll have another cup of coffee from your nice coffee machine and talk about it, OK?'

When Emma unlocked the door a feeling of apprehension nearly swamped her. How would she cope with another move, maybe having to store furniture, finding something else to live, looking for jobs? The list in her head seemed to recur endlessly and it was hard to decide how to prioritise things. It's the shock of it all, she thought, as Fletcher went to stand by the door to the balcony while she made coffee.

If it had been one thing or the other, I wouldn't have this terrible feeling of indecision, I'd be able to deal with it one thing at a time, but now I feel threatened as if my whole life will be upended and everything that means stability might be in ruins. I worked hard to re-set my life, and now this, like a slap in the face.

Before they sat down with their coffee, Emma got

her list from the previous day and held it up for Fletcher to see. 'Yesterday I went through all possible employers of librarians, the university, the high schools – both here and in the region, the museum and so on, but I found no jobs advertised on their websites, or on the online job agency sites either.'

She passed the list across to Fletcher. 'So, I phoned all those on the list, barring two where I couldn't speak to someone in authority.' She made a face and added, 'There are no vacancies for librarians and none coming up in the near future. Though a couple of places took my number and asked me to send a CV – in case they need me later.'

Instead of reading the list or commenting on what she had told him, Fletcher said, 'Can I see the letter they gave you, and a copy of your employment agreement? Not that I'm any kind of expert, but there might be something you've missed. What's the name of the HR yokel who gave you the letter.'

'McLean,' said Emma. 'He didn't tell me his first name. Just an admin type guy, I think, about thirty.'

While Fletcher read the papers she gave him, Emma went to stand by the window, deep in thought about what kind of job she might be able to get. Something with a reasonable level of pay and where her qualification would be useful in some way. But nothing came to her, and she told herself to get used to the idea of losing the apartment.

'Listen,' said Fletcher after a while. 'This

employment agreement mentions something that could be a veiled reference to that phrase McLean used – "last hired, first fired". I think he said it that way because it's their internal slang for it. Here it says in paragraph 6.4.2 that in the interest of fairness when a redundancy must be made, care will be taken to protect the interests of long-serving employees who had devoted time and effort to safeguard the interests of their employer.'

He looked expectantly at Emma and when she said nothing, he shook his head. 'What a dumb-fuck thing to do - use internal lingo when he's delivering a redundancy letter. What did you say to him?'

'I asked if my qualification had no value and pointed out that if left Cora as the only fully qualified person, and then I asked if I could see the figures. You know, how much the overspend was compared to the budget. He didn't know, said it was up to the finance department to decide if they release things like that.'

'The letter says your employment ends in a fortnight, but here you are – not at work, the day after you were given notice. I hope you didn't just say you'd leave immediately! You could lose your unused holiday pay.'

She could see how worried he was now and thought how lucky she was to have him here, such a solid friend and so helpful. 'I'm not as green as I'm cabbage looking, Fletch - I asked for this and got it, well I got two things. Have a look.'

He took her phone and read the two emails from the manager of the council's HR department: the first confirming she would be paid for the notice period even if she left immediately and that her holiday pay would be paid out regardless, and the second with her reference attached.

'And the reference contains the thing I asked for, saying I had been made redundant for financial reasons and through no fault of my own.'

When Fletcher left he hugged her tight and held her for a moment. 'Kia kaha, girl!' he said and let her go. 'I know you're strong, but this might require some extra strength, and if it does, you know I'm here for you. And may I add that if I wasn't gay, I'd be after you like a shot – pretty and clever! Who could ask for anything more?'

Emma laughed and kissed his cheek. 'That's possibly the most flattering thing anyone's ever said to me – thank you!'

Chapter 11

A week later, Emma's phone woke up when her phone buzzed. 'Hi,' said Anne, sounding totally awake and alert though it was only quarter past six. 'Sorry if I woke you up, but I've got something to tell you. Can we meet after work? I'll come to your place if you don't mind.'

'Of course,' said Emma with a feeling of slight apprehension. 'I'll be here and …'

'Sorry, have to go,' said Anne, and Emma heard a boy's voice shouting something in the background. 'I've got to be quick – he's got to be at school at seven, his class is going on a three-day school camp. See you later!'

When Emma opened the door for Anne at half past five, she knew immediately that Anne was excited about something. Her face is like a canvas, thought Emma, everything she feels is painted on it, no need for a label to explain it. She was curious about what was so urgent, but she didn't ask in case it ruined Anne's pleasure in surprising her. Asking to come to Emma's place instead of meeting down-town was very unusual, so maybe what she had to say was private or emotional.

'What would you like to drink?' she asked as Anne sat down on the sofa and put her bag on the floor. 'I've got some white wine in the fridge, or we can have coffee.'

'Wine, please. You might need it when you hear what I've found out.'

Emma put their glasses on the coffee table and tried to look calm. 'Obviously you're excited about something. Did that handsome guy ask you out? You know, the one you say looks like George Clooney and I always say, is that George Clooney, the window cleaner from Tauranga?'

Anne drank some of her wine and her expression changed to serious, more serious than Emma had ever seen her before, and she felt instantly alarmed.

'You weren't made redundant – it was rigged, and you were effectively sacked.'

'What? Why do you think that?'

Anne gave her a grim smile. 'I don't just think it – I heard Cora on the phone. You know how she's one of those annoying people who raise their voice when they're on the phone? She was in her office, but she hadn't closed the door properly, it was open just a crack, and I was coming down the passage from the back door with a box of books that just got delivered. But when I heard your name I stopped and listened.'

Emma's mind went into overdrive, ideas about having the redundancy revoked, confronting Cora, or suing the City Council flitted through her brain with breakneck speed. 'What exactly did she say?'

'That's the problem,' said Anne. 'The conversation must have been going on for a while, so I have to guess a little. But the gist of what I heard probably means that she had just said to someone that she wasn't pleased to lose the only other fully qualified person on her staff. And then she said, "I don't give a shit who you were doing a favour for – it's not right, and it will serve you right if she files a complaint about constructive dismissal." And then she listened for a while. and her comes the crucial bit. Cora said, "And you can leave my brother out of it, he's outgrown all that rubbish". What do you think it means?'

They looked at each other across the table, and Emma took a big swallow of her wine and tried to sort out if her first reaction could really be right. It seemed a bit far-fetched, but what else could it be? Aloud she said, 'Who do you think she was talking to? That's the most important thing, isn't it? Knowing who it was, might put us on the right track.'

'I've no idea and I don't think it's important at all. Obviously someone at the council, but my guess would be the **HR** manager. What I want to know is if you talked to anyone else apart from me in the last few weeks, I mean about the letter you found – in public.'

Ah, thought Emma, we're on the same page here. 'Only one person, very recently. I had lunch with an old student friend. Remember that day when I took a long lunch hour? We were at the French Bistro, and we sat in one of the booths. I picked the one right at the end deliberately, so we'd get some privacy because we had some old misunderstandings from years ago to sort out. I was showing her photos of the letter and the envelope on my phone, and we were talking about it, and then I realised someone had come along without me noticing and was sitting right behind Nadine.'

'That's what I thought it might be! I wondered if someone had overheard you talking about it.' Anne took another sip of wine and leaned back. 'Let's say this person has some kind of link to that Brotherhood, the group we speculated that maybe Cora's brother was involved with. And then that gets passed on to someone on the council – or maybe the person who sat behind you works at the council – maybe they are linked to the Brotherhood too. Endless options for how this got to someone who pulled the plug on your job.'

'You're right,' said Emma. 'So, some key person at the council calls Cora and ask what she knows about this letter I found and what she knows about me. And result is that the person who's highest on the food chain of those involved gets on to the HR manager and asks them to get rid of me as a favour.'

'But *why?*' asked Anne after a few moments while they both thought about this theory. 'Why would they bother? I mean, what does it matter to someone down here who's linked to that group? Just talking about the letter isn't a good reason, is it? It's old history. I mean, I *do* think those things are linked, but why is it important? I just don't get it.'

Emma thought fast about how much she might safely tell Anne. She trusted her, but could she be persuaded to keep her mouth shut about everything to do with this, or was it such a tempting story that she wouldn't be able to resist telling someone else? After a long pause Emma said seriously, 'Will you swear not to mention what I'm going to tell you to anyone, not a single soul. Swear on your mother's grave.'

'I can't do that,' said Anne reasonably. 'My mum's alive and kicking – literally – she goes to low-kick cancan classes for older women on Wednesdays.'

'Ah well, just swear then, but I'm *very* serious about this. It's could turn to custard for me if rumours got out and were linked to me. I'm in enough trouble already and I don't want to be sued.'

When Anne left half an hour later, she stopped on the doorstep and promised once again to tell nobody. 'I totally see your point,' she said. The least said the better, until it's a fact instead of an assumption. And if it's true that Miller guy will be outed sooner or later.'

. . .

The call from Fletcher came at the end of an afternoon spent applying for jobs not directly related to libraries, but some where her diploma in information studies might be useful, and others where two-and-a bit years of science and maths might fit in. She had updated her CV the previous day, carefully working on the wording relating to the redundancy to make sure it didn't read as an excuse and added her reference from the library as part of the file.

'Hi,' he said when she picked up the call. 'Not good news, I'm afraid. I know you said you didn't want to talk to Catriona about this, trying to avoid too much agonising – which I totally understand – but she might have some other ideas for you to try. Our lawyer says it's perfectly possible to demand information about the budget from the city council, but it will take time – they never like to give out details, and they often try to stall the process, so it's no immediate help. If that budget excuse can be demonstrated to be fake, then you'll need mediation with an employment lawyer present. If you take it to the employment court it won't come up for close to three years.'

'Really?' asked Emma, surprised by the wait time. 'Why? Do they have that many cases?'

Fletcher said, 'Exactly what I asked, but it's a combination of the covid-19 effect and the number of employment disputes arising from people losing their jobs during and since the pandemic. Anyway, the court is way behind, so whatever you decide to do, you must get a job with good pay in the meantime, so you don't have to lose the flat. Or move to another city if there's a proper library job available, of course, that's the obvious option.'

'I know. I was thinking about that last night when I applied for jobs in Christchurch and Nelson and Blenheim – not library jobs, I couldn't find any, just other jobs. I think the best thing is to wait a little while and see if I can get a reasonable job here.'

'And sadly, nothing at all coming up here at the lodge,' said Fletcher. 'Nobody's indicated they're leaving, and I can't invent a new position. I wish I could, but it wouldn't get past head office, staffing is a monthly reporting requirement.'

The following three weeks became a marathon of trying to stay hopeful and not spend too much time gloomily contemplating what her future might turn into. Hardest of all was making a decision about whether she would tell friends and family that she had not only lost her job, but that she was now on the brink of having to give up her flat. Without even thinking about it she could predict what would happen. Her mother would call more frequently, endlessly suggest new ideas, offer to pay for the move back to the North Island where there would be opportunities and try to cheer her up. But in the North Island there would also be greater numbers of applicants for all those jobs, thought Emma, and therefore less chance of getting one of them, and accommodation would probably be more expensive too. Her father would worry and tell her to come and live in Australia, using the same reason he kept repeating after the accident: "getting as far away as possible from the site of trauma is a good thing". And in addition, the endless and repetitive enquiries and commiserations from her friends would drag her down. Talking about the same dispiriting things over and over was exactly the thing that had nearly broken her once before, and however well-meaning people were, constantly reverting to it was debilitating.

By the last days in April, it was becoming clear that the jobs Emma had thought she might be suitable for with the various components of training she had, would not be given to her. For some strange reason the fact that she had her full librarian qualification seemed to be regarded as a negative quality. Over-qualified was a term used in several rejection letters, but it was a concept she had never before been aware of; having more qualifications than a job required apparently made her an unsuitable employee.

With less than a month before the deadline for agreeing to the increase in rent, Emma resigned herself to giving up the flat. Her holiday pay from the library had now run out and she was living on her savings. She clung to the hope that she would land a good job before she had to make a decision, but it seemed unlikely after a long month of trying. In the meantime, she took the job she least wanted as a dishwasher in a Mexican style restaurant in one of the suburbs.

Am I spoilt or is this one of the worst jobs in the world? thought Emma as she drove home at half past eleven one nightg. The side room off the restaurant kitchen where the dishes were washed, was cramped and steamy. Endless piles of dishes arrived, and it didn't seem to matter how fast she tried to work, the pace didn't slow down until after ten most nights. She had never realised how things worked behind the scenes, just taken for granted that a lot of machinery was involved, but the reality was very different.

How could she have been so ignorant and unimaginative, she thought, as she went up in the lift, drooping with exhaustion. The different parts of the job interlocked and overlapped in a stressful and heavy cycle of repetitive tasks. Scraping food remains off plates into a bin, stacking them to rough wash by hand, then putting them into a machine that did the final clean at very high temperatures and dried them in a few minutes. Raising the hood of the machine and releasing a cloud of hot steam, lifting out a heavy basket full of plates, so wide she could only just lift it. Then putting it to one side and lifting another one into the machine, it went on and on. Then a basket with glasses, then emptying baskets and putting heavy stacks of plates on the shelf that opened into the kitchen. Backbreaking was the only word for it, but the worst was the damage to her hands, particularly scrubbing of pots and pans by hand, a job that had to be done in between other tasks right through the evenings.

Having coffee or a glass of wine with Anne now and then had been the best part of her life since the sacking, though she now never ordered a pastry and never had more than one glass of wine. When they met at their usual café at lunchtime at the end of May, after not seeing each other for a couple of weeks, the first thing Anne said was, 'My God! What happened to your hands? Is it an allergy?'

'It's dermatitis,' said Emma and felt grateful that she had one person apart from Fletcher she could be honest with. 'I've got some cream for it.'

'Detergent rash from that dreadful job, I suppose – I can't believe you couldn't get anything better!' Anne reached across the table for Emma's hand. 'You poor thing - it's awful, your skin is actually blistering, and it must hurt like hell. Can't you wear gloves?'

'I've just started doing that now, but they make the job quite difficult – hard to keep hold of some things when they are slippery.' Emma looked at her hands and sighed. 'But the gloves make my hands perspire and it's just as bad as the detergent – being constantly damp irritates the rash and it never gets any better, just stays the same.'

'Have you tried barrier cream? You know that stuff that puts a kind of coating on your skin, so water just runs off.'

'Oh yes, I tried that fairly early on, but it washes off – and when I wear gloves my skin gets so damp inside the gloves from perspiration that the cream just melts off. And now I can't put it on at all, the cream is too hard to spread, and my skin is too damaged.'

'You've got to leave! This is ghastly,' said Anne. 'It hurts just to look at you. I don't know how you've managed that job for so long with your hands like this. You must apply for the unemployment benefit.'

'I know,' said Emma. 'I will.' She should have done it a few weeks ago, but her stupid pride and sense of independence has made her want to exhaust all other possibilities first.

Chapter 12

When Emma arrived early during food prep time, the restaurant owner seemed genuinely upset when she told him she could only work to the end of that week. 'Oh no! You've been such a great worker. Are you sure? I could pay you another dollar per hour if it's the pay that's the trouble.'

She didn't respond in words, she just held her hands out and he looked startled, 'Ouch! That's awful – you should have told me, but you never said anything.'

'There is nothing you can do that I haven't done already. I've tried everything, barrier cream, rubber gloves, vinyl gloves – the doctor said nothing's going to stop this until I stop being a dishwasher. Once it's taken hold even getting hot and sweaty makes it worse.'

'You're such a good worker,' he said again when she left. 'I don't want to lose you - I'll call you if a waitressing job becomes vacant.'

The next evening she decided to give herself a treat and walked ten minutes to her favourite Thai take-away shop, where she hadn't been for some weeks.

'Welcome back!' said the woman behind the counter. 'How are you? Have you been away?'

'I've been busy, and now I might be moving,' said Emma and on in impulse added, 'My flat is going to cost too much, the rent is going up, so I've got to find something cheaper, but there's very little to be had. The university students took everything available at the beginning of the year.'

Ten minutes later she picked up her little box of food and paid, but before she got to the door the woman said, 'Hang on, wait a moment. If you don't mind something very, very simple I could ask my neighbour about his container. He got it a few years ago for a relative who was a student, but it's empty now.'

Emma stopped with her hand on the door. 'A container — like a shipping container? Wouldn't that be like living in a black cave?'

'I don't think this one is too bad — it's been converted. Arnold, that's the old man who owns it, showed it to me when I first got to know him. I sometimes bring home a meal for him, he's very old and lives on his own, so we often chat. The container has a little wooden step and a big glass ranch slider door, so it kind of looks a bit like a little house. And I'm sure he wouldn't charge you much to live there. Maybe it would be OK until you find another flat?'

Emma walked home with her little box of Thai food and the note with Arnold's address in her pocket and thought of how lucky it was she had told the Thai woman about having to leave her flat. Not the sort of thing she would normally tell someone she only vaguely knew, but it might be the luckiest thing that had come her way for a while.

The following morning, Emma looked up Arnold's address on Google Earth and found that Sandy Road was on the opposite site of the city and meandered out into the countryside. Arnold lived at the end closest to town, and as she sat there working out how to get there by the simplest route, she noticed that she could see the container in the satellite image. There was the house, close to the road and what looked like a track running under large trees alongside the garden. Behind the house, in a field with two clumps of trees, sat a rectangular box with a small hut or something similar beside it.

She set out at mid-morning the following day, as she had no wish to disturb an old man in his dressing gown and sat in the car for a moment studying the place before she got out. Even without knowing that somebody very old lived there, she would have been able to guess at the age of the owner. It had an old-fashioned look to it, as if nothing had been altered or modernised for many decades, but it was tidy, and the lawn was mowed. The garage was the old single-car version with double doors to unlock and fold open, the kind of garage nobody had built since the 1950's. When Arnold opened the front door, she understood why the Thai woman had said she sometimes brought him a meal. He looked ancient, gaunt and stooped and leaning on a walking frame, but his eyes were bright and alert.

'Yes?' he said, his voice hoarse and gravelly. 'Can I help you?'

'I've come to ask if I could rent your container. Your neighbour, the Thai lady, gave me your address.'

'Come in,' he said, turned labouriously and moved started down the hall. 'Close the door behind you and come into the kitchen. Would you like a cup of tea?'

'I'd love a cup of tea if it isn't too much trouble,' said Emma and followed his slow progress down a long passage to the back of the house.

Ten minutes later they were sitting at the table in Arnold's kitchen with mugs of tea and biscuits. 'I can't go shopping,' he said and pushed the biscuit packet towards her. 'Helpers from the welfare do my shopping and deliver it, but the kind of biscuits they buy depends on who's doing the shopping. This time is chocolate wheaten, which I like.'

'So do I – particularly these that have the milk

chocolate topping instead of the dark kind,' said Emma.

'Me too, I don't like the dark chocolate either. So, you want to live in the container? Are you sure?' He coughed. 'It's very simple, so you might not like it. There's no toilet, just an outdoor privy in a little shed next to it. My great-grandson who lived there for a couple of years used to come into the house and have a bath now and then, and he had showers at his rugby club. But it's primitive, not like what you're used to probably.'

'I don't mind,' said Emma and took a biscuit. 'I have to give up my flat because the rent's going up and I also lost my job, and there's nothing at a reasonable rent available. I've been trying to find something for a couple of months. The students have taken everything cheap, and I've only got four weeks now until I have to get out of my flat. I'm pretty desperate, to tell you the truth.'

'You're welcome,' said the old man and coughed hard for a moment. 'If you can cope with living in a metal box, you can have it for free, just pay me a bit for the power. There's a long power cord from my laundry, a real outdoor cord like a cable that runs along the top of the fence on the side.' He pointed out the window and coughed again. 'I had a whole cut in the metal side for it to go into the container, and my great-grandson might even have left that thing I put in for him to use - one of those gadgets so you can plug several things at the same time. That was in the days when I could still go to the shops. But now I can't even walk down the track. I worked all my life in a quarry and the dust ruined my lungs, walking is beyond me now. But when you've had your tea I'll give you the key and you can go and have a look by yourself.'

Having made this long speech, he coughed again for a couple of minutes, drank some tea and said, 'I'd only charge you twenty dollars a week or something, just for the extra on my power bill. You'll need a good heater, that metal box will be freezing.'

They finished their tea and Emma walked down the shady track with the key he had given her, desperately hoping the container would not be totally awful. It was such a godsend, and she was prepared to put up with nearly anything in the hope that it wouldn't be for very long. The container was raised off the ground on concrete blocks and had a wide ranch-slider set in the centre of the long side with a wooden step like a little platform outside the door. When she slid the door open the first thing that struck her was how chilly it was inside even on a sunny day.

She could live there, she thought, and stood for a few minutes, mentally working out what would fit in, what she needed and how to arrange things to best effect. Yes, it was possible, but she must get a heater and probably some fleece blankets and maybe something to put on the bare wooden floor.

She took a quick peep into the primitive toilet

arrangement in the little hut, which was just what she had expected: an oval hole in a wooden bench and a half-used roll of yellowing toilet paper on a string hanging from a nail.

'I'll take it, thanks,' she told Arnold when she returned the key, 'I'll be I touch when I've sorted out my life and made some arrangements for the furniture that won't fit in the container. I'll take your phone number so I can tell you when I'm moving in.'

The next three weeks went by in a blur of activity interspersed with nights when Emma woke up every two or three hours, either worrying or trying to mentally prioritise her tasks for the next day. She spent one disturbed night agonising about what to tell people, and who to tell, or whether she should tell anyone at all. In her mind her present situation felt like personal failure, as if she had done something wrong, let herself down and ended up in a mess. The mere thought of pity and commiserations, friends always asking if she was managing, and what the container was like to live in, or offering help - she felt overwhelmed just thinking about it. There could be nothing worse than having to constantly discuss and listen to encouragement or simplistic suggestions. It was easy to imagine the range of comments she would be forced to interact with, and she knew she simply couldn't cope with it. Tragedy in the past has taught her that she was best left to process things without too much input from others. She must find some way of concealing what her life had turned into until she had changed things for the better but working out how to do it required a lot of internal discussion.

Her immediate priority was to update her budget, so she could work out how long her savings would last, taking into account how much moving and storing excess furniture would cost. She searched websites and added to her budget the cost of a heater, two fleece blankets and a large, but cheap floor rug, because somehow she must create an environment which felt marginally civilised even if it was in a bleak metal box. It would be like living in a cave, yes, but she would try to make it a civilised cave. She would need to hire a moving firm to take her things to a storage facility and then the rest to the container, work she knew she could not do herself and which would be her biggest expense. Storage would be an ongoing cost, but it couldn't be helped and after some disappointing quotes from big companies she found a small, private facility on Facebook. It was nothing more than a very long metal shed behind a house on the western side of town, where the owner had partitioned off spaces separated by wooden frames and steel mesh. She went to see it and thought for half the price of a big, secure storage facility, it was worth the risk. The man who owned it pointed out that he had installed security cameras both outside and inside, and Emma told him it was perfect for what she needed, and she would take his last space. She changed her contents insurance to "all household goods being stored at a private property with CCTV and alarm system" and hoped nothing would happen to her possessions.

Not knowing if she would be able to find a job in the near future made her feel insecure in a way she never had before. Having nothing in reserve for unexpected expenses was a terrifying prospect and her savings would not cushion her for long. The only thing she could do to counter financial disaster was to sell the car and get an older and cheaper one despite the obvious long-term drawbacks. Once again she told herself that she must be sensible and apply for the unemployment benefit, and once again she put it off.

When she finally moved out, three days before her lease ran out, she was pleased with what she had achieved. She drove behind the removal company's truck to the storage place where the men helped her pack her belongings into the small space in the most efficient way, then from there to the container. She saw the look the men exchanged when they realised how she was going to live, and that look told her that she had made the right decision that tedious night when she made up her mind not to tell anyone about the container until she was in a normal life again.

The day of the move was sunny and warm for the time of year with no hint of the icy winds from the high mountains that often came sweeping down over the city in winter. With the few pieces of furniture inside the container and a pile of boxes on the ground outside, Emma waved goodbye to the movers and started to organise herself. She unrolled the floor rug at one end to create a bedroom space with a bedside table beside the bed, which left enough of the rug to place her armchair on with the coffee table beside it, though the table was on the bare board floor.

After an hour and a half, she had labouriously moved her big bookshelf a bit further along the opposite wall from the armchair and arranged her clothes and books on the shelves. When she shelves were full, two boxes of clothes remained on the floor, but on the whole she was pleased with what she had achieved. She unpacked the electric heater and put it between the armchair and her bed and pushed the little dining table into the far corner.

By mid-afternoon she had unpacked what she thought of as her kitchen; microwave oven, electric jug and toaster lined up on the dining table in the corner, an extension cord to the table from the multi-socket power board and some basic food supplies in a box under the table.

Lunch time, she said out loud, and opened a can of mushroom soup, which she had with two pieces of toast while reading the news on her phone. It was only then she realised that with no internet connection she could only use her laptop by pairing it with her phone. She got up and made sure the charger and cable for the phone were where she thought she had packed them, set up everything for easy access on the end of the coffee table and went back to reading.

The next realisation came after lunch, when she took her soup bowl to the table in the corner and found she had overlooked the need for water and something to wash both dishes and her body in. She already knew she could have a shower for a couple of dollars downtown at the Information Centre, but for basic daily ablutions she needed not only a bowl but a supply of water as well.

When Emma knocked on Arnold's door he was delighted to see her again and invited her in to tell him how the move had gone. Over another cup of tea, she described how she had organised herself in the container and told him how she had forgotten about something to do the washing up in.

'I've still got the big plastic container Nigel used,' he said. 'Not that I had any use for it, but I hate waste and I thought one day someone might want it and you can have it.' He coughed violently and drank some tea.

'So, what you do is this.' He half rose and pointed out the kitchen window. 'You take the wheelbarrow – see it out there, leaning against the side of the garage? You put the big plastic container on it and fill it with the hose from the tap just below the window. I think Jeremy said it holds twenty litres, it's a decent size. And then you wheel it down the track to the container and put it up on something – it's got tap on the side so you can fill things from it. And mind you don't fill it right up or you won't be able to lift it.'

She thanked him, asked if he needed anything from the shops, and headed downtown. When she returned an hour later she had acquired a plastic bucket for laundry, two plastic basins, one plastic jug, dish washing things and two rechargeable camping lanterns.

By the time the early winter dusk set in, Emma was organised and locked herself in. She pulled the curtain across the sliding door, turned on the standard lamp by her chair and sat down to contemplate her new home. But within minutes she got up and looked up at the large round hole in the wall where the power cord came in just above her chair. Cold air streamed in and sank to the floor where it gradually replaced the warm air from the fan heater at her feet.

'Bubble wrap', she said to herself. 'There's some in the box I had the kitchen gadgets in – that will do it. I don't have any gaffer tape, but I'll do a temporary fix.'

She got the bubble wrap out of the box in the back of her car and sliced it into a long, narrow strips, which she wrapped around the cord, layer after layer until she could push it along the cord into the hole to seal it. As soon as she sat down again she instantly felt the difference and feeling proud of her improvised problem solving she spent the evening studying. Then she turned everything off apart from a lantern on her bedside table and climbed into bed.

The cold woke her at two in the morning; she

spread the second big fleece blanket on the bed, put socks on and went back to bed telling herself that it was no worse than winter camping.

The next four weeks made Emma realise how the things one never thought of in what she regarded as normal life, became tiresome and difficult when you lived like she did. She thought with compassion of parents who had to bring up children in this kind of life; the endless chores of fetching water, boiling water in the electric jug to get warm water for washing and washing up, the time-consuming chore of taking linen and towels to the laundromat and waiting for the washing machine and the dryer to run through their cycles.

It rained a lot and snowed three times, and the track and the area around the container became muddy and soft, so shoes had to be kicked off on the little wooden platform, and then put inside to avoid them sitting outside in the rain. After one or two irritating events, she bought a pair of rubber boots and rummaged through the copse of trees along the track until she found two short broken branches which she pushed deep into the wet ground, so she had a place to hang her boots upside down.

Every night when she went to bed she put on socks and a jumper and stayed warm by training herself to lie still under the duvet she had tucked in around her body with no gaps to let chilly air in.

Two or three times a week she spent the afternoon in a café with free wifi, sitting at a table with her laptop from just before lunch until they closed at four, eating a cheap lunch and having a cup of coffee a couple of hours later. This was where she could study in comfort and talk to Catriona and her mother on Skype on her phone. They thought she was in her lunch hour, and she was careful not to let slip anything about her situation. Gradually routines evolved; she used the showers at the Information Centre three times a week and started leaving her toiletries and towel on the back seat of the car instead of bringing them inside, the lunch in the café replaced dinner on the days she went there and at home in the container she read a lot.

In the second week of living there she traded her low mileage Honda for a five years older Toyota and was able to deposit $3600 in her slowly emptying bank account. Always in the back of her mind was the thought that she might have to move back to the North Island and somehow money for that move must be kept as a final reserve. Applying for jobs whenever she saw one got no results because the inexplicable stigma of having a useless qualification applied nearly across the board. She thought that students probably got the unskilled jobs, and she could see the logic of it from an employer's point of view.

The fact that her only face-to-face meetings were with Anne and Fletcher, made Emma feel isolated and abandoned, as if life had left her behind and was moving on without her. She could go for three days without saying a single word to another person apart from the staff in the café; the only people she felt comfortable to talk to were her mother and Catriona, and once Nadine. She told everyone without exception that she had found a tiny studio flat behind a house just outside the town boundary, and that she was looking for an apartment she could afford. To her mother she said she was prepared to wait until the end of the academic year, and not to worry, she was perfectly fine where she was. Sometimes she thought with longing of the nice, warm library, but she couldn't bring herself to go there to use the public computers and face questions about her situation.

Chapter 13

Later Emma would think back on what it was that gave her the idea of going to the picnic area beside the river on a cold day in late winter, however fine it was. In the summer the spot that local people referred to as "the rocks" was a popular place to go in the weekends with children and a picnic, to swim in the summer-shallows of slow-moving water warmed by the sun. To go there in winter on an impulse was perhaps not what most people would do, but several things conspired to plant the idea in her mind.

The idea started when one of the library staff posted two photos on social media: one of her three children sitting on top of a gigantic round rock, the size of a small house, dressed in swimsuits and smiling widely in bright sunshine, the second photo was the view through her kitchen window of the garden obscured by pouring rain. The text read "Can't wait for summer!" Several people had commented and posted their own photos of the rocks, a lot of them with comments about the current miserable weather and how much they longed to be back by the river. And then, as if fate had designed a plan, she heard the rocks mentioned twice within a week, first at the petrol station and then at the supermarket check-out.

On a sunny August Saturday afternoon, desperate to escape the confines of the cold container and have a change of scene, Emma picked up her phone and an apple, drove through the city centre and set out on the road northwest. In the past she had looked down on the river picnic spot from the highway when she was heading back to town. The road was carved out of the side of a hill and from some of the bends it was possible to see the parking area and the river, but not the rocks themselves, which were hidden by trees, and now it seemed a pleasant goal for a short road trip.

She spotted the signpost as she came around a bend and worried about the black SUV that was following too close, she indicated and pulled quickly off on the shoulder opposite the little access road to let the SUV pass. There was only one car in the parking area, just ready to drive off when she got out of her car. She gestured a greeting, and the man in the passenger seat rolled down his window, as his wife put the car in reverse. 'Well worth it!' he said, and then they were gone.

The river was high with rushing water foaming

around big rocks, much deeper than in the summer photos on Facebook. Emma spent a couple of minutes admiring the giant rocks and taking photos before she headed back downstream to where the river had created a deep bay in the bank close to the parking area. Standing on a flat rock on the edge of the curve carved out by the river, she studied the surprisingly deep water, unaffected by the strong current that swept past in the river itself. This must be wonderful in the summer, she thought, no wonder it's such a popular spot. The natural pool in front of her would be perfect for swimming, and the river would have less water, so it would flow much slower. Deep in the pool a surprisingly large fish hovered stationary, facing into the slight current with the sun glinting off its speckled back.

Behind her tyres crunched on the gravel access road and when she heard two car doors slam shut she turned. A black SUV had parked beside her car, two men were coming towards her, and suddenly she felt apprehensive. There was something purposeful and vaguely threatening in the way they walked side by side directly towards her. They looked business-like, as if they were on a mission, and she thought she should go back to her car, but they were between her and the parking area. As they closed in on her, they took a few rapid steps and split up in a manoeuvre that looked as if they had decided on it in advance. Now she was effectively hemmed in, with one man on each side.

Before she could react, one man took hold of her arm, and the other said, his voice hard and cold, 'This is a warning and an ultimatum. We know that you're antifa and what you're up to, but you're playing with fire. The brotherhood defends its own and you have two choices, it's entirely up to you. You can stop talking about the letter and hand it over to us, and also your phone - we know you have photos of it. You can't fight the brotherhood — we're more powerful than you can imagine. If you refuse to do what we say, we'll break you.'

The man on her other side shook her and his fingers dug into her arm. 'And when we say break, we mean break — one leg at a time, then one arm at a time and then we throw you in this handy river.'

In her mind the words "handy river" was the trigger, the thing that snapped her out of the feeling of the breathless terror that had gripped her when they arrived beside her. Arguing or trying to run would be useless, and her brain assessed in a split second how far she was from the water's edge and that two step would be enough. Her right foot responded to the thought, made itself ready to push her forward, her right hand reached across and tore at the hand grasping her arm, she used her whole weight to swing her body forward and her arm pulled free. She felt the other man's hand try to take hold of her sweatshirt at the same moment that her left foot took her weight and pushed, then she let herself fall forward into the deep water.

For a couple of seconds, the icy shock took her breath away and her heart missed a beat, then she was swimming, gasping and frantically trying to overcome the drag of her clothes, clumsily doing breaststroke across the still water towards the fast-flowing river itself. Then suddenly the powerful current took hold of her body and rolled her over, tumbling her and dragging her under. Time ceased to matter, the only reality was panic and her throat constricting to prevent water flooding her lungs. Then a hard, sharp pain in her chest as if her heart was being squeezed, and when she knew she could hold her breath no longer she was suddenly the right way up with her face just above the water, arms paddling desperately to keep her afloat as the river carried her rapidly downstream.

Blinking water out of her eyes she spotted a willow on the opposite bank with a branch hanging low over the water. She tried frantically to get across to it, but the current swept her downstream faster than she could swim across the flow. She began to despair of being able to stay afloat much longer with the weight of her clothes pulling her down, and then the current unexpectedly brough her nearly within reach of the bank. She made a final desperate effort and got closer still, then a rock at the edge of the water abruptly and painfully stopped her.

She lay draped over the rock with her legs still in the strong pull of the current and tried to catch her breath, her heart hammering in her chest. But fear kicked in again and she knew she must get up and disappear into the trees before those men saw her from the other side. They would probably try to see where she went, to see if the river had completely carried her away, or if she had drowned or got ashore somewhere. She turned her head and scanned the opposite bank, but there was nobody in sight. She dragged herself further up, got unsteadily to her feet and took a deep breath.

Five minutes later she stopped her stumbling progress in a clump of manuka trees, leaned against a tree trunk and vomited violently before she sank to her knees on the ground.

Chapter 14

Emma had no idea how far she was from the road that ran on this side of the river, a road she had never travelled and only vaguely noticed on maps. She pulled her supposedly waterproof phone from her back pocket to look at Google maps and nearly cried with relief when it instantly lit up, but her heart sank when she noticed there was no signal. She pushed the phone back into her wet pocket and trudged on, hoping she wasn't too far from the road. She knew it came in at angle, getting closer to the river as it headed south, until it crossed a bridge before joining the main road.

Dripping wet and shivering, she tried to picture a map of the roads and the river and work out the best direction to go to get to the road. The increasingly strong wind hit her left side with icy force and that would give her a bearing. So long as that wind came at her from the left, she was walking in a straight line, whether that would take her towards the road or not. It was better than walking in circles, the only rational idea she could muster.

After slowly struggling through dense native bush for forty minutes, with her strength nearly depleted and shivering despite the exercise, she reached the road. She clambered through a deep ditch and headed south in the near dusk of the late winter afternoon, now cooling rapidly. Her clothes were no longer dripping, but still heavy with water and she was very cold.

While she had battled her way through the bush, negotiating fallen tree trunks and trying to keep on a straight course with the wind on her left cheek, she had tried to think of ways to keep warm. But apart from the physical act of walking and wrapping her arms around her chest she could think of nothing. The chilly wind penetrated her wet clothes and eroded her body heat. Keep moving, she told herself, don't stop and don't sit down. Even with the little she knew about hypothermia, she understood that sitting down for a rest might be the end of her, she might not have the strength to get up and could fall asleep there on the verge of the road.

Half an hour later she heard a car coming up behind her and turned to look, though if it was a man or two men she would ignore them even if they offered her a ride. She trudged on as the car slowed down beside her, the passenger side window rolled down and a man's voice said, 'Are you OK?'

'I'm fine, thanks,' she said, swung a quick glance his way and noted he was alone in the car. She looked ahead again along the uneven verge she was walking on and hoped this man wouldn't turn out to be some kind of trouble.

'Would you like a ride into town?'

'No, thank you.'

'Why are you wet?'

'I swam across the river.'

Oh, for God's sake, would this bloody man never give up? She still didn't look at him, just continue walking with the car cruising slowly beside her. She had had enough of strange men today and there was no knowing if this one wasn't after her too. Maybe those two at the river had called in reinforcements, someone to cruise up and down on this side of the river. If he was another Brotherhood guy he would know why she was wet, but maybe asking her was a ploy to make her trust him. Her focus was fixed on keeping going because she knew she was close to the extreme edge of exhaustion now, and the bridge had become a beacon of hope in her mind. She had to get there and refused to think of how far it was from the bridge to where her car was. Probably the best thing would be to hitch a ride back to town in a car with a woman in it, as soon as she was back on the main road, she thought, and retrieve her car another day. But keeping going until she crossed the bridge and got to the main road was the most important thing because her strength was waning, and she knew that if she sat down for a rest she would not have the strength to get up again.

And constantly in the back of her exhausted mind ideas and speculation circled endlessly, like static interfering with logic and decision making. Would those men still be at the river where her car was parked, after all this time? What if they had immobilised the car somehow? Or set fire to it? But surely they would have left by now, perhaps after searching for an hour or two, then assuming she had drowned? She stuffed her freezing hands into the pockets of her wet sweatshirt simply to get them out of the wind and shuddered at the feel of the cold, wet fabric.

'Hey, listen!' said the voice from the car, which she had nearly forgotten while she concentrated on her thoughts. 'I'm only trying to help you. And you look very cold. I really don't think you should be on this lonely road at dusk, and dark comes early now. It's not safe, anything could happen.'

She turned her head then and looked straight in the window at him for the first time and realised he had turned on the interior light so she could see him. 'Like some stranger might drive alongside me and try to persuade me to get in his car?'

The driver leaned further over, and serious brown eyes studied her. 'Yeah, probably a bit like that, but I'm only concerned about your safety. You'd be perfectly safe in the car. I can show you ID if you like.'

Seriously irritated now and feeling colder by the

minute despite walking a fast as her strength allowed, Emma said sarcastically, 'And your ID proves that you're trustworthy? Like your occupation is stated as Safe and Reliable Male, I suppose?'

To her surprise he laughed then, genuinely amused and said, 'OK, then - I'll stop and get my ID out for you to see, it's in my jacket on the back seat.'

She continued without reply, leaving the car behind her on the shoulder of the road, and then a minute later he caught up again, but now he was on foot.

'Here,' he said and held out a black folding wallet as they continued walking side by side. She took it from him and said, before she opened it, 'Did you lock the car?'

Out of the corner of her eye she saw him shake his head very slowly from side to side as if he found her comment hard to believe. 'You're a real character, aren't you? Would you please open it and check I'm OK, so we can sort this situation out.'

And then she knew, and it nearly made her laugh. Of course, only a police officer would be so persistent and ask so many questions instead of just driving off, and that term "this situation" was probably classic cop speak. She stopped, opened the wallet and there was his photo ID card and on the opposite side a shield fastened into the leather, blue and gold enamel with the entwined letters NZP surrounded by a circle of leaves of some kind, with Det. Sergeant, New Zealand Police below it. She struggled to get her phone out of her damp back pocket, and with hands shaking with cold, took a photo of his ID balanced on one hand before she handed the wallet back and noticed his look of surprise.

'It's waterproof,' she said, pretending to assume he was wondering about the phone. 'I tested it as soon as I got out of the water in case I needed to call for help – but there's no reception around here.' Stuff him, she thought, I can be as careful as I like, I'm not feeling safe at all, anyone could be after me.

He made no comment, just pulled a beanie from his pocket, stepped in front of her and pulled it down over her head, right down as far as it would go. She opened her mouth to protest, but nothing came out. Instantly the aching chill of the wind on her damp hair ceased to be a torment, and she stood stunned and slightly disorientated, unsure of what to say or do. Exhaustion enveloped her in a fog of indecision and her mind was blank.

'Well? Are you going to accept a ride? Your lips are blue and you're shivering, you're probably borderline hypothermic – that river is mostly snowmelt from the mountains at this time of the year.'

She gave in. The thought of a warm car, getting out of the wind and sitting down outweighed her previous fears. They walked back to his car in silence and in Emma's mind rational thought slowly trickled back. There was a slight possibility that this cop was a member of the Brotherhood and had been sent out to find her, but if that was the case he wouldn't have worried about how cold she was, and he certainly wouldn't have put a beanie on her head. She got into the car and sat immobile while tremors shook her body. He started the car and turned the heater up high before he reached over and did her seatbelt up, and the blast of hot air was like slipping into a hot bath, she relaxed and closed her eyes, and let her body melt deeper into the seat. After a moment she realised the car was still stationary on the verge of the road. She opened her eyes and saw he was watching her.

'Now then,' he said. 'Where are we going? Do you live somewhere near here?'

'I live in town – I just came out here to look at the river.'

'And then you had an irresistible impulse to go for a swim in your clothes? Did someone throw you in? Were you assaulted?'

She remained silent for a long moment, while a new worry appeared out of nowhere and warned her to be careful; she must weigh up how much could she safely reveal. The last thing she wanted was for this guy to decide he had to start some kind of investigation that might make her life more difficult than it already was. She recalled that harsh warning to tell nobody, and what would happen to her if she did. But how could she explain it to this man without him taking her straight to the police station? And that would probably be his first reaction and also the most dangerous thing that could happen, something that might bring instant retribution.

Finally, after a silence he had made no attempt to break, she said, 'It's a long story but I was …' Her voice petered out because she still couldn't think what to say.

'Yes, you were what?'

'A couple of people followed me,' she said slowly. 'They were trying to persuade me to keep silent about something – well not persuading exactly, they were threatening me. I thought they might beat me up, or worse, so I jumped in the river and swam to the other side.'

'Where were you?'

'At that picnic spot, you know, the place with the big round rocks that people climb up on in the summer.' A strong shudder shook her, and she paused for a moment. 'I think the river carried me quite far, but it was hard to judge because it flowed much faster than I'd expected, and I was underwater some of the time. And this road – I've never been on it, so I didn't know how far away I was from the main road.'

'Jesus, girl!' he exclaimed. 'The trouble you could have been in – the worst! You could have drowned or been lost in the bush, frozen to death. You must have walked a long way before you came out onto this road then, the river's way over to the side of us. I presume your car is still on the other side?'

He asked no further questions while she sat beside him, limp and exhausted as they drove south. She still had her phone in her hand, now she put it on the centre console, bent to undo her trainers and pulled her wet socks off. Her toes were so cold they looked pale blue and felt as if they belonged to someone else, numb with cold. Studying the heater controls, she re-directed the air on her side to blow on her feet as well as her body and sighed when hot air filled the footwell. She knew he was glancing at her now and then, but he said nothing and fifteen minutes later they crossed the bridge and turned onto the main road north, the stretch she had driven up earlier that afternoon. When she realised how long it would have taken her to walk there, she wondered if she would even have made it that far and thought that possibly this stranger had saved her life.

The picnic area was deserted, and her car was where she had parked it, neatly squared up against the logs forming a barrier in front of the grassed area where the fixed barbecues sat like humped beasts in the gloom.

'Thank you for being so persistent,' she said and unclipped her seatbelt. 'That was very kind of you - more than kind.' She bent and with some difficulty put her wet shoes on, stuffed the socks into her pocket and got out.

Still silent, he got out on his side and walked around her car, looking carefully at it, tried the doorhandle and said, 'I hope you've got your key. Was that long scratch there before?' He pointed at the rear door, and she smiled at his concern, as she got her key out of her right-hand jeans pocket with a hand that now felt swollen and stiff.

'Someone's supermarket trolley got away from them in the wind last week. I won't fix it – this car isn't worth it.'

'Would you mind getting back into my car for a few moments? It's warm there and I want to ask about a couple of things.'

'No, I want to go home now.' She got into her car and started the engine, but he walked around behind her, effectively stopping her reversing, got into the passenger seat and reached out to put his hand on top of hers on the gear shift.

'Hang on a minute, will you?' His hand held hers in a warm grip, and she gave in.

'OK – what do you want to know?' But she knew, of course, that the mention of men having threatened her was something he couldn't ignore.

'I'm sorry to hold you up, but I'm still worried about this. Keep the engine running so the car warms up.'

She turned her head to look at him. 'Oh, for God's sake, would you just let it go! I don't want a fuss made - my life is difficult enough already, and if the police get involved it will just make things worse. Would you please get out and let me go home?'

'Just two or three questions,' he said calmly. 'And I won't do anything official if you really don't want it, I promise – provided there's nothing illegal involved. I can see you're scared of this becoming official, but I need to understand why. Just answer me and satisfy my curiosity.'

'OK, then.' This was the last straw, but he seemed as immovable as a rock and the fastest way to get rid of him was to do what he said, so she could go home.

'The two people who threatened you were males?'

'Yes.'

'Do you know them?'

'No.'

'Do you know something illegal they have done – or that someone else has done, someone they're protecting?'

'No, not illegal.'

'What is it then? You said they wanted to silence you – so it must be something significant.'

Oh shit, she thought tiredly, did I actually say that? How stupid to let that slip. 'It's not a crime, it's more like a reputation thing they don't want the public to know – something I know about someone else, not about them.' She thought for a moment and added. 'Potentially very damaging.'

'Where did you jump into the river?'

She stared at him for a moment, confused. 'Where? Just down there to the left. I was standing there looking at a fish in that deep part where there's no current, it's like a bay in the riverbank. They got here about ten minutes after me. They must have followed me because they came to warn me – it wasn't random.'

He sat silent with frown lines between his black eyebrows, looking down towards the river where she could see the rock she had stood on, in the beam of light from her headlights. She was just about to ask him again to get out when his attention switched back to her.

'So, the last they would have seen of you would have been as you were swept away by the current and disappeared around that bend and out of sight?'

'Yes, probably,' she said and knew what he was thinking. Suddenly, thinking of how terrifying it had been when the river took hold of her, she felt an urge to tell him, to make someone understand how it had felt, as if sharing the terror and panic might help her. A strange and unexpected need to know that somebody apart from herself understood what it had been like.

'The cold took me by surprise,' she said rapidly, trying to keep her teeth from chattering. 'I threw myself in to get away and the impact of the cold of the water was like a physical blow.' Involuntarily she put her hand on her chest. 'It felt as if my heart stopped, the shock of that intense cold, brutal. And then once I was out in the main part of the river, the current rolled me over and I went right under, right down so I could feel the rocks on the bottom. I didn't know if I could get back up and take a breath and ...' Her voice was breaking and the words "I thought I was going to die" became impossible to voice; she shuddered at the memory.

'You're safe now,' he said, and his hand, which she hadn't realised was still holding hers on the gear shift, grasped hers more firmly. 'So, they probably waited for a while, decided you had drowned and left. Or is it possible they saw you re-surfacing?'

'I don't know.' She felt calmer now and considered for a moment, while the heater gradually warmed the car and made her feel drowsy. 'They might have. When I got my head above water, I noticed a willow on the other side with a big branch growing out over the water, and I tried to get across to grab hold of it, but I was swept downstream too fast. I was much further down river when I finally managed to get to the other side, quite a long way down.'

'Wait here, would you – I'll just be a minute or two. Lock the doors around you and keep that heater going full blast, and leave your headlights on, please. And I mean it, do *not* leave until I come back!'

He got out and paused until he heard the click of the central locking, and she watched him walk along the edge of the water and around the deep pool until he disappeared into the trees. She sat there thinking that she could leave, he couldn't possibly stop her, but maybe he had those flashing lights mounted in his car and then he might chase her and catch her, which would be embarrassing. She decided on the path of least resistance and waited.

After a few minutes he returned and knocked on the window for her to unlock the car, got in and half-turned in the seat to look at her. 'It's nearly too dark to see, but the light from the headlights filters through to the trees and I couldn't see that willow, so it must be further around the bend. I think it's unlikely they saw you get out of the river if you were swept around the bend.'

They looked at each other for a long silent moment, and Emma knew they were thinking the same thing; if those men assumed she had drowned, then for the moment she was safe.

'I'll drive behind you back to town. And promise me you'll stop if you feel wobbly, don't take any risks - you look exhausted.'

Chapter 15

While they were on the main road she glanced at the rear vision mirror now and then, and it was comforting to know he was there. His dipped lights remained the same distance behind her the whole way, but when they drove into the city she stopped checking. There were too many distractions, and she was too tired, she had to concentrate hard on driving safely. Assuming he had dropped away, she stopped looking in the mirror as she skirted around the business centre instead of going through it. She kinked left then right into the suburbs that she thought of as 'the dark side' and wound her way around to Arnold's place just outside the speed limit, where horticultural land took over from suburbs.

Before she turned into the half-overgrown dirt track down the left side of his house, she turned her headlights off and switched to parking lights. It was dark now and Arnold went to bed very early; she didn't want to disturb him by letting her headlights sweep into his bedroom.

After parking the car beside the container, she let herself in and pulled the curtains across the glass ranch slider before she lit her two lanterns. A moment later there was a knock, and she slid her hand around the edge of the curtain to check the door was locked before she looked out. That persistent man had followed her all the way home and now he was at her door. But why? Was he going to try to persuade her to report the assault? Quickly she pulled the curtain right back, bent down and engaged the bolt in the bottom track that prevented the door sliding back more than a few inches, well aware that he could see what she was doing, and slid it open a crack.

'Yes?'

'Can I come in? Just for five minutes? I want to check you're safe here.'

'Five minutes? This place is so small it takes ten seconds to check it out. If I let you in you'll just stay and ask hundreds of questions. And I'm so *tired!*' She heard her voice starting to break and cursed how vulnerable she suddenly felt, as if her battery was nearly empty and she had no strength to cope with his questions.

'OK,' he said, still calm, which made her feel rude and ungrateful in equal parts. 'I apologise – I'll leave. I have no right to invade your home, but I feel very concerned about you.'

'Oh no, no - I'm sorry!' she said quickly. 'I'm just running out of steam, and I'm so grateful to you. Of course, you can come in.' She bent and pulled the bolt up from the track, and slid the door fully open. He came in and looked around. 'No windows?'

'No, it's just a shipping container. Nothing fancy.'

She saw it through his eyes, the freezing cold room, metal walls painted white, the bed at one end and just a few pieces of furniture, but still not leaving a lot of room. Her clothes hanging on the little freestanding rail she had bought in the charity shop, the tall bookshelf crammed full of books and folded clothes, and the tiny wooden chair painted white with a flowery seat cushion. His gaze swept around the space, took everything in, and fastened on the table with the electric jug and the microwave oven, paused on the extension cord coming in through the wall with bubble-wrap sealing the hole. It's his trained eye, she thought, he's used to making a fast but complete inventory. Well, now he knows everything about how I live.

Still shivering from cold and shock, still terrified by what had happened at the river, her determination to appear composed suddenly evaporated. Exhaustion claimed her and her knees buckled, then everything went dark. When she came to she was lying on her bed, and he was taking her shoes off, then his hand touched her thigh and she flinched.

'Let's get those jeans off, they're still damp,' he said and calmly proceeded to unzip her and pull the jeans off. 'Now sit up.' He helped her raise herself and took her sweatshirt off, the way you do with a small child, one arm at a time and then over the head. Suddenly a fit of strong tremors hit and before he asked, she pointed. 'Sweater,' she said, her teeth chattering. 'On the chair – and leggings.'

With his help she got into the warm, dry clothes without getting off the bed, then he covered her with the duvet and tucked it tight around her body and shoulders, right up to her neck. He must have folded it back before he lifted her onto the bed, she thought, closed her eyes and felt herself slip into sleep despite how cold she was.

'Ari, hi,' he said a moment later, and her eyes flew open to see him standing beside her bed with a phone to his ear.

'Listen, if someone's got very cold by first getting soaked and then walking a long way in wet clothes in this freezing wind, and I mean cold to the point of uncontrollable trembling and blue lips - and then they faint. Is it ED or what?'

He listened for a moment, and Emma closed her eyes again. 'OK, hold on will you.'

He put the phone on the bedside table and sat down on the edge of the bed, pulled her right arm out from under the covers and took her pulse before he tucked her arm in again and picked up the phone.

'Her pulse seems pretty normal, and her skin is warmish, I suppose - and she's not shivering as badly as she was, probably from getting really warmed up in the car. Yes, she's got dry clothes on now and she's tucked into bed. Ah, yes, I can do that. Thanks, Ari!'

'Hot drink, she said, and extra warmth.' He moved away and she heard him check the jug, so she roused herself and said, 'There's water in that big container and the power is always on – the extension cord, I mean.'

'Have you got a hot water bottle, or any empty bottles?'

'No.' She tried to get up, but he heard the movement and returned to the bed and pushed her down, pulled the duvet up around her shoulders again and said, 'You stay right where you are, this is serious!'

Ten minutes later she was sitting up with another sweater he had found on her armchair draped over her shoulders, the beanie was back on her head, and he was handing her a mug of hot tea. 'Hold it with both hands now. I don't want you scalding yourself on top of everything else, and it will warm up your hands too.'

She sipped the tea and felt the warmth run down inside her body like a stream of comfort. Neither of them said anything; she was concentrating on holding the mug and he was watching her closely, and then his phone buzzed.

'Hi – yeah ok, hang on a minute.'

He pushed his hand under the covers and felt one

of her feet. 'No, they're a little warmer than when I took her shoes off, I think. OK, will do – and if not? Right, thanks, Ari.'

Emma slid down into the bed again and he took the half-empty mug out of her hand just in time. Her eyes were shutting and this time she didn't try to resist. Within seconds she was asleep.

When she woke up she had no idea what time it was. He had turned off the two lanterns and plugged in the standard lamp, and now he was sitting in her armchair with a book. He didn't notice that she was awake and for the first time since he had slowed his car beside her on the road, she really studied him. About forty, maybe a couple of years less, she thought, solid, very solid, and not handsome but not ugly either. She squinted to see if she could work out what he was reading and failed, then he put the book face down on the table and turned towards her, as if he could feel her intense scrutiny.

'Ah, you're awake. Are you hungry? Have you got any food here?'

'I'm not hungry,' she said without sitting up, warm and snug now in her bed. 'And it's probably late now. You should go home and have something to eat.'

'No way,' he said. 'It's you I'm thinking about. You need nourishment and I'm going nowhere. I have nutbars and chocolate in my car – I always do. I've eaten a couple already and I made myself a mug of coffee. But you need something after losing a load of calories by being so cold for so long. '

'There's food in the box under the table – just canned stuff, and bread and eggs. I don't have a fridge. I'll heat some soup up.'

He got up and handed her a KitKat bar and put a hand on her shoulder. 'Stay where you are and start with this.'

Emma sat up and realised her feet felt funny, she lifted the quilt and looked at her feet. Socks! He'd put her thick woollen socks on her feet, and she hadn't even noticed. 'Socks? How did that happen?'

'I saw them on the shelf, so I put them on to warm you up a bit faster. Your feet were still cold, when I checked, like my sister said I had to every hour. Apparently feet are important because they're so far from your heart – they take ages to warm up.' He smiled. 'You didn't even stir.'

'Was that your sister you were talking to? Ari?'

'Yeah, Ariana, she's a nurse. Now then, what do you want to eat? Soups sounds OK, but perhaps something a bit more substantial? I'll heat something up for you.'

'What time is it?'

He pulled his phone out and laughed. 'God! It's just after midnight. Doesn't time fly when you're reading? It must be two hours since I checked your toes. Do your feet feel warm?'

She started up at him standing there, and he seemed to fill the limited space left by her furniture and belongings. Feeling disorientated and nearly frightened, she wondered how she could have slept for hours, not felt his hands on her feet or taking her pulse or whatever else he might have done. And at the same time, she wondered if she would have survived the night if he hadn't been there. She pictured herself lying on the floor, in cold, damp clothes as the temperature dropped closer and closer to zero, the way it had a few times this winter, and the thought made her shudder.

'My feet are nice and warm now, thanks. But I'm so sorry I've ruined your evening. I can't believe I slept so long – and you've been sitting there all that time.'

'No worries, I've been reading. But I must say I'd like to know your name now. It's weird not knowing who you are.'

'Oh, sorry - my name is Emma. And I'd like to know yours too,' she said and smiled at how silly this was, to not know each other's names after all that had gone before. 'I couldn't see what it said on that ID card, but I do have a photo of it on my phone, of course, so I could look it up.'

'It's Ben, youngest son and all that. So, what are we eating?'

When he was ready to leave at half past one, after a dinner of baked beans on toast, he put her number in his phone, got up from the armchair and sat down on the edge of the bed, very serious.

'Now don't argue with me, Emma - this is *not* negotiable. If you can't agree to this — agree so I believe you really mean it — then I'll stay here all night.' He paused and she waited, silent and slightly worried again about what he might feel obliged to do. 'Before I let this drop, I want some more information from you, and it's *not* to make it a formal police matter, but there's something wrong here - I can nearly smell it. You said it's not illegal but connected to someone's reputation.' He shook his head when she tried to interrupt him. 'Hang on a moment - so if it's serious enough for someone to send thugs to scare you, then it needs looking into. Something's going on either with you or around you, or you've come across something you don't want to tell me about. But having seen what your bookshelf is full of, I don't think living in a cold container in a field is what you're used to, so I assume things have been going wrong in your life. So, two questions. Are you involved with drugs in any shape or form? Are you a user or do you know people who deal drugs?'

Outraged, she sat up straight and glared at him. 'Of course, I don't have anything to do with drugs! Do I look like a druggie — or a dealer? How could you even *think* a thing like that?'

She was so angry she was close to tears, but Ben stayed where he was on the edge of the bed without moving and said calmly, 'No, I don't think that, but it's a question that springs to mind when I hear about thugs following and threatening people. It's usually about unpaid debts, and what people look like has nothing to do with it. You'd be surprised at the number of middle-class people you see in the street every day who have a drug habit – and those who can't afford it end up owing nasty people money. Same with gambling addicts who gamble on borrowed money.'

She kept her eyes on his, intent on finding out if he was telling her the truth. 'Do you believe me?'

'Absolutely,' he said comfortably, as if they were discussing the weather. 'I do for some reason, don't quite know why, I don't know you after all. Now then, do you have to go to work tomorrow – I mean, today?'

'I haven't got a job right now, I'm trying to find one, but …' Her voice tapered off; telling this stranger felt like an admission of total failure, as if she lacked determination or focus, unable to achieve a way of making even a simple living.

'But what?'

'Oh, it's complicated, just let it lie. I'm nearly unemployable, I think. First I lost my real job, then I had to leave one, then I couldn't get another. I should probably move on. I seem to have got on the wrong side of the wrong people now.'

She could see that her reply had made him even more curious, and she regretted having told him she felt unemployable. He gave her a hard look and made no comment.

'Now get up and lock the door behind me and then

get straight into bed again. And remember - this is not finished. I'll be back tomorrow morning, or rather, this morning. Will you promise to stay at home until I get here, so we can talk?'

'OK, I promise.' She got out of bed and stood holding the sliding door as he stepped out and said, 'Thank you for looking after me for such a long time. If you hadn't come along I would probably have died on that road. I'm very sorry I was so rude earlier.'

'I'll see you later today,' was all he said. She watched him walk down the long, narrow track to the road, nearly invisible under the trees, locked the door and thought that he must have parked on the road. What a kind man! And what on earth did his partner or wife think he was doing all this time, but he probably called or texted while I was out like a light. If I didn't feel him putting socks on me, I wouldn't have heard him make a call.

When she lit a lantern and turned the standard lamp off, she looked at the book lying open face down on the table and smiled; he had been reading The Martian, one of her favourite books. She folded the corner of the page and closed the book, turned the heater off and got back into bed.

Chapter 16

Just before midday Emma's phone beeped with a message: "I'll be at your place in half an hour if that's OK, will bring sandwiches and coffee, Ben" and she replied, "Thank you."

Quickly she got out of the jumper she still had on over the now dried T-shirt from yesterday and had a quick but chilly wash with a washcloth before she put on her warmest merino jumper with a high neck. Despite feeling warm on the outside, there was still a remnant of cold deep inside her, as if something in the centre of her body had stored so much cold that it would take time to warm up again. Clean panties, jeans, socks and her old trainers, and she was ready. She brushed her hair and put yesterday's wet shoes outside on the wooden step in the sun, bundled the washing into the plastic bucket by the door and sat down in the open doorway, relishing the warmth from the sun.

'Now then,' said Ben when they had eaten the sandwiches he had brought. He used that calm, decisive command voice he sometimes used, which Emma thought must be his police officer voice, the voice that had told her to get straight back into bed last night. It made her laugh inside, to think that she had been treated to those calm-voiced orders, as if she were a non-threatening criminal or a child, as if he didn't already know that she was capable of ignoring him and doing whatever she wanted to do, whatever he said. It's like a little game we play, she thought, one of those funny things that develop between people, but it's never happened as fast as this before – very strange.

'What I want you to do now is pack clothes and stuff for a few days, take anything valuable you keep here and come with me.'

'What?!' The idea that she would go to some unknown location, with a man, however kind, and whom she had only known one day was outrageous. 'Where? I can't just go off with you like that! And why aren't you at work anyway?'

'I just came off a double period of night shifts on Friday, so I have extra time off. And I'm not abducting you, I'm just taking you to a safe place for a couple of days.'

His eyes remained steady on hers as he spoke, and she wondered what he had found out or heard that made him feel this was necessary. And how could he possibly have found out anything relevant, when he didn't know her full name or any details about what had been going on in her life? Or had he looked up her car registration? But she wasn't going anywhere without more information, and even then she might not go. Command voice or not, she must make decisions for herself.

'Where is this place? Is it your sister's? I can't just go with you and not know where I'm going!'

'Very sensible,' he said and suddenly his eyes crinkled in a smile. 'Usually, it's not a good idea to go off with men you don't know, but in this case it's OK. I can't take you to Ari's place because she hasn't got room for you, it's only a small townhouse. They've got kids and her husband snores so badly she sometimes sleeps on the fold-out couch in the living room downstairs, so not even that's free.'

Emma looked unflinchingly at him and waited, hoping they weren't going to end up having an argument about this, but she must know where she was going. In the back of her mind, she admitted to herself that at the same time as she insisted being told where he wanted to take her, she was scared he would get so fed up with her that he left without her, gave up on her because she was too difficult to deal with.

When he arrived that morning she had experienced

a sense of relief so intense it had shocked her. He brought with him a feeling of solid safety, and though she would never admit it, she knew that for the moment she needed his support. Right from the start the container hadn't felt like a very safe place to live, set in a field some way behind the nearest house and the only person close by a very old man who was slightly deaf. And after what had happened now, it felt positively unsafe, as if she must barricade herself inside in case those men found out where she lived. Unlikely, she knew, but she had no idea what they already knew about her.

'I'll take you to my place. You'll be safe there and comfortable, and I won't bother you. This place is horrendous, cold and damp - it's unhealthy and unsafe and I don't want you to stay here.'

She baulked at the thought of going home with him and reminded herself of the risk that somehow, for some reason yet to come, her problem would become official police business, and if that happened she could become exposed to exactly those she was trying to avoid. But during a long silence, while he waited patiently and she weighed up the pros and cons and tried to reach a balanced decision, one thing became clear in her mind. Though it was very unlikely that the Brotherhood guys would find out where she lived, she knew that if they did, she would be in serious trouble. What I'll do, she thought, is go with him and just avoid telling him anything he mustn't know, anything that could prompt him to start some kind of investigation, that's all.

'Thank you,' she said. 'It's very kind of you, but won't your family object to a total stranger moving into the guest room or whatever? I wouldn't want to cause any trouble.'

'I live alone, so there's no family to worry about. You can be as private as you like at my place, forget it's mine and just regard it as a safe house. You won't be in my way, and you don't have to do anything. This is about you, not about me.'

It didn't take Emma long to pack some clothes into her canvas zipper bag, but then she came to a halt in the middle of the room, as she tried to think what to put the rest into.

'Is there a problem?' asked Ben, who had sat quietly in her armchair reading the book he had left on the table in the night. 'Aren't you sure how much to take?'

'Oh, no – the problem is that I know exactly what I want to take, but I don't know what to put it in. My suitcases and other bags are in the storage unit with my furniture, there's so little room here and I didn't think I'd need them.'

The look he flicked her way told her he was intrigued by this, but he didn't comment, just got up and said, 'I've got two of those collapsible boxes in the back of the car – I'll get them.'

She was putting things on the bed when she heard the car just outside and moments later he put the two boxes on the floor beside the bed and looked down at what she had assembled so far.

'Are you a student? Those books look like university texts.'

She straightened up from where she was crouching beside the bookshelf. 'I'm doing an external degree – picking up where I left off a couple of years ago.'

She added three books to the pile already on the bed and mentally checked the items: laptop and charger, textbooks, the old book she got from the library, phone charger, her two large notebooks, pens and pencils, her diary, the Latin grammar, toothbrush and Kindle.

'That's it,' she said and started packing it neatly into the folding boxes. 'I must go and see Arnold before we leave, or he'll worry about where I am. That's the guy I rent the container from - he lives in the house by the road. He's very old, nearly ninety, and he doesn't like change and upheavals, so I'll just tell him you're a friend who's taking me to the bus station, and say I'll be away for a few days.'

He slid a sideways glance at her but made no comment, and when she returned from Arnold's place he had put her things in the car.

'I put that bucket of wet clothes in as well,' he said. 'Took another liberty with your privacy, you can wash them at my place. They'll probably get mouldy if you leave them here.'

She was about to lock the door, when he said, 'Wait

a moment - is that little bag of clothes enough? You didn't pack a jacket or a beanie, or any toiletries.'

God, he's observant, she thought, amused at the thought of a policeman noticing the lack of toiletries. But he's a detective, so I suppose checking everything is second nature.

'Your detective skills are impressive, but there's method in my madness. All that stuff lives in my car, so I'll just get it out when we get to your place. I can't shower here, so there's no point having those things inside cluttering up the place.'

'You can't take the car, not if you told the guy next door I'm taking you to the bus station,' he said reasonably. 'It's got to stay here. Put some the extra stuff in the second folding box, it's nearly empty.'

She knew what he was thinking; if the Brotherhood guys came here and asked Arnold where she was, things must fit with the story she had told him. Quickly she picked up another couple of changes of clothes and her jacket, put them in the half-empty box in the car and went back into the container one last time. With some difficulty she managed to lock the door, with Ben's beanie and the book he had been reading clasped under one arm and holding the little child's chair with the flowery cushion resting on top of it. 'Can we put this in the car, please?'

'Of course.' He opened the rear door without comment, and she placed the chair carefully so the legs wouldn't damage the leather upholstery of the back seat and threw the other things on the floor before getting the last things she needed out of her own car.

It's interesting how he manages to refrain from asking questions or even comment when he chooses, she thought, as they drove away, but when he scents some kind of evasion he's like a terrier, he refuses to let go, but quietly, no raised voice, no display of impatience.

Ben's house surprised Emma, though she wasn't sure why. There was no reason at all why a single man couldn't live in a pretty, nineteen-thirties bungalow with a full-width veranda along the front and a white picket fence. The kind of house that might have been on the lid of a chocolate box way back when images of kittens and pretty cottages were common decorations.

The house was in Hunter Street, half-way up the slope of the hill locally referred to as "the second hill" and looked out over a neighbourhood on the lower slopes that had probably mostly been built in the same era. Emma was unfamiliar with the suburb, but she knew it was sought after and probably expensive. Had he been married and kept the house? Had his partner or wife left him? Suddenly she thought how odd this was, that despite knowing practically nothing about him, she had still agreed to come and stay at his house, and it struck her as one of the most uncharacteristic things she had ever done.

'First door on the right is yours,' said Ben and stood to one side after unlocking the door, before he went back to the car to get the last of her luggage.

The room was perfectly tidy, and the bed was made, but it had the look of a room that had rarely if ever been used. The only furniture was a queen size bed and a kitchen chair, the walls were a pretty, greyish pale green, but there were no pictures, no mirror and nothing that reflected the owner's personality. Intrigued she wondered what the rest of the house looked like, particularly the living-room and his own bedroom, the two rooms most likely to give her a clue to him as a person. Behind her, Ben came in with the second box and the little chair, the seat cushion tucked under his arm.

'Make yourself at home.' He put the things he carried down and gestured. 'The bathroom is between this room and mine, and I've put some towels in there for you. Why don't you have shower or a bath and enjoy some running hot water after yesterday's soaking? I'll bring a little table for you to have beside the bed – and make use of the wardrobe, it's got shelves on one side. Take your time and tell me if you need anything.'

But for some reason the sudden change of environment left her feeling lost. The implications of his insistence that she mustn't stay in the container, the way he sometimes didn't show what he was thinking and the remnant of fear from yesterday, all these factors combined to immobilise her. When he appeared in the doorway again a few moments later she was still standing in the middle of the room, indecisive, as if she didn't know what to do.

'Now, go and do whatever you want to do in the bathroom – for as long as you want. There's a warm dressing gown on the back of the door, my niece leaves it here for when she stays the night. And then we'll have coffee. I know it's not long since lunch, but I bought some nice biscuits when I was shopping this morning.'

As if he could sense how hesitant she felt, he remained in the doorway, and impelled into action by his steady gaze, she gathered up her toiletries, went into the bathroom and closed the door.

Three quarters of an hour later, she came out, still glowing from a long hot bath, the most luxurious feeling she had experienced for a long time. With her hair still damp and slowly curling as it dried, the way it always did if she didn't brush or blow-dry it straight, she stood hesitant and silent by the kitchen table and watched him making coffee and rip a packet of biscuits open, but not with his teeth she noted approvingly. She took the mug he passed to her and sat down.

'Now then,' he said, and she smiled inwardly at this habitual way of his to start to a conversation, which was becoming very familiar. 'I'd like to ask some questions, just to understand your situation – nothing formal or official, just between friends.'

She looked carefully at his face before she replied,

because it was important to her to know he meant it, that he wasn't just using a stock phrase to put her at ease, to possibly make her reveal more than she wanted to. 'OK, ask me whatever you like.'

With certain reservations, she told herself, because there were some things she probably would never tell him, now or later.

'First up – why do you have a storage unit?'

The question took her by surprise; she had been expecting searching questions about the details she hadn't told him yesterday, what had really caused the Brotherhood to come after her and to whose reputation she was a threat. In her head she had a list of things she might need to avoid hesitating about and to somehow deflect, or possibly simply refuse to discuss, but the storage unit was not on the list.

'When I had to give up my flat, when I lost my job and couldn't find another I couldn't find anything reasonable that I could afford. It was just about the time my lease was rolling over and the rent was going up, so I had to move. And then I heard of Arnold and his sleep-out which was empty – not ideal as you've pointed out, but cheap. I'm actually only paying for the power. It's obviously not big enough for all the stuff from a quite spacious flat, so I had to find a place to store my things.' She paused for a moment to imagine what he would ask next. 'It's not a real storage facility and it doesn't have security gates and things - but it's behind a house in a suburb that seems decent. Just a huge, long shed with wooden frames with wire netting dividing it into a few separate spaces. And once again, the rent is minimal, so I can afford it - until my money runs out, anyway.'

'OK, and what are you studying? The books you brought are about maths and physics, but there was a Latin grammar too – a very eclectic mix of subjects.'

He smiled and she had to smile back. However much she didn't want to tell him all her secrets, she had to admit that what he had asked so far was disarmingly harmless. The way his eyes crinkled at the corners was very endearing, and she was beginning to get used to the shorthand of how he expressed himself. Or perhaps it wasn't shorthand, just very direct, with no lead-in and no unnecessary words. Was this how he conducted interviews, this way of asking questions so it became nearly impossible not to answer? I'll have to study him, she thought, and work out if it's a strategy or just the way he is.

But aloud she said, 'The Latin grammar isn't a real book, it's a fake. It's a box that looks like a bound book, and you've got to know the trick to open it. It's quite clever, it can sit in a bookshelf and look like a boring old book. It's got my most precious things inside, some jewellery, my passport, my credit card and some photos and papers that I wanted to keep handy.'

'Very clever – I never heard of those before.' He grinned and took a biscuit from the packet between them on the table and pushed it towards her. 'Who would even look at a Latin grammar, much less steal it? Have a biscuit, you look as if you've lost weight. Where did you work and why did you lose your job? Because I presume that's what happened?'

How does he know I've lost weight? she thought. This is weird, I must figure it out, or I might ask him later. Another item on my list of mysteries to unravel about this guy, who might be irritating at times, but extremely interesting too.

'I worked at the library,' she said and reached for a biscuit. 'I was made redundant, but it wasn't …'

God, she thought, I nearly told him too much already and look at him now, his eyes are drilling holes in my head. He instantly picked up on that. Was it a change of expression or what I said?

'Was it a sham redundancy?' he asked. 'Did they use it as an excuse to get rid of you? What had you done?'

'I had done *nothing*!' She was suddenly furious and cast caution to the winds. 'Absolutely nothing! I didn't know it wasn't true at first, this was back at the start of April. They said their budget had been over-spent and it was a case of last hired, first fired. And I fell for it. But it was done as a favour to someone in a position of power, it had nothing to do with their damn budget. I found out afterwards and worked out how and why it had happened – and I know I'm right.'

'How do you know that?'

And then all at once, despite her earlier warnings to

herself to be cautious, despite the trouble it might lead to for her personally if he thought it needed to be formally investigated, she decided to tell him. She was tired of this game of hide and seek, the strangely truncated conversations they kept having, and sick of not being able to tell anyone what had happened. Fletcher and Anne knew, but they never talked about it now, whereas she had it constantly in the back of her mind and sometimes dreamed about it. She needed to tell him and make him understand it, not for sympathy but to document what had happened to her. Fully aware that she might regret this impulse at some stage in the future, she sat up straighter and said, 'It's a very long story. I *will* tell you the whole thing, if you promise not to make anything official out of it, because after what happened at the river, I truly believe I'll be in danger if you do.'

She kept her eyes focused on him because she must pick up any hint of hesitation. This must be a genuine promise or things could go desperately wrong.

But his response was immediate. 'Of course,' he said, as if this was a given that needed no thought. 'I already promised I wouldn't do that. Why don't we go and sit in the living room so we can be comfortable while you tell me? Bring your coffee and tell me when you need a refill – or a cup of tea, perhaps?'

Tea? she thought, first we have coffee and now the refill might be *tea*? Curiouser and curiouser.

Chapter 17

The living room instantly made her feel comfortable and relaxed. Emma looked around and wondered if he had decided the colour scheme himself or if someone else had done it, maybe an ex-wife or a partner, or even a decorator. Furniture in muted shades of dull thunder-cloud blue, a smattering of pale yellow, pale green and dull pink in the patterned cushions scattered on the sofa, two striking modern paintings and a shelving unit with books and a TV.

'Now then,' he said again when she sat down on the sofa and picked up her mug, with Ben in what she supposed was his usual armchair on the opposite side of the low table. 'Start at the beginning and let's have it – I'm very curious now.'

'I bought a book,' she said. 'A very old book about mathematics donated to the library years ago. It was on the for-sale shelf where we, I mean where they put books they're weeding out, for various reasons, mostly because of wear and tear. I was interested in the writer - I'd read about him, and I bought it for a dollar. When I had a proper look at home I saw that it had a note on the front flyleaf that said it had been donated to the library by a local man's relatives after his death along with other books. On the reverse side of the flyleaf was a name, not in the same writing or with the same pen as the note. The name was Hermann S. spelled with the two n's – the way the Germans spell it.'

She drank some coffee and mapped out in her mind how to explain the conclusions she had come before she continued, but first she wanted to explain the book. 'And by the way, the book was written by GH Hardy, now dead, the man who among other things developed a way, over a hundred years ago, to untangle genetic population odds via maths, which is still in use today.' She paused, thought, and added, 'Long before DNA and all that, of course – but there was extensive genetic research going on via experiments and observational studies, the continuation of that whole branch of science that started with Mendel.'

She put the mug back on the table and thought that maybe she shouldn't have told him all those details about Hardy, but it was so interesting, and then she tried to remember where she had got to. She was still very tired, and she must concentrate on making this coherent and clear.

'Inside the book, I found a letter in an envelope addressed to Mr Harry Webber - written by a man who signed himself Gerhart, but the letter started with "Dear Hermann". So right off I was interested. I mean, one name on the front of the envelope and a different one at the top of the letter, which was also the name on the reverse side of the flyleaf of the book. So, someone had changed their name from a German name and a surname starting with an S, to Harry Webber and surprisingly he had written what I presume was his read name in the book. Which seemed odd, but maybe that's what he did with books. We'll never know.' She paused for a moment, tried to force her mind to stay on topic. 'And it was an interesting letter too, very interesting in the modern context of the white supremacy movement and today's fascists.'

She took a sip her coffee while she thought of how to continue to make the story logical and Ben remained silent, as he often did, just waiting.

'Then I noticed that the sender's name on the back of the envelope wasn't Gerhart, he was called Gerald Miller, the same name as the aspiring mayoral candidate in Auckland. So, there was second man who had left a German name behind and adopted a very ordinary English one. The letter was written in nineteen ninety-one.'

Ben said, 'But that guy Miller, who's hoping to be the next mayor of Auckland, he was born in New Zealand, I remember reading an article about how he got his money and it mentioned where he went to school. I read up on it because I'd never heard of him before and wondered how he got so wealthy and was suddenly so well-known. And anyway, he's not nearly old enough to have written that letter more than thirty years ago.'

'I know, but listen,' said Emma, inexplicably feeling invigorated after his response, keen to map it out for him so it made sense. She found herself leaning slightly forward, as if it would make what she was about to tell him more credible. 'I think the letter was written by his grandfather, and that *he* wasn't originally called Gerald Miller, though he came to New Zealand under that name, on a UK passport. I think he was really Gerhart Mueller spelled with the German "u" with a so-called umlaut over it, which means "miller". His friend Harry Webber, as he is called on the front of the envelope, was probably a German called Hermann Schmidt, who arrived on the same date as Gerhart/Gerald, also on a UK passport and on the same ship from Argentina - in 1950.'

'Jesus Christ!' said Ben and sat up straight. 'How the hell did you find all that out? And how much is assumption?'

'I found the letter in February, so ages before most of the mayoral candidates were starting to appear in the press, apart from Gerald Miller who was very busy making noise and generating a lot of interest in the media, so he already had a distinct media profile and a big following on social media even then. He was that thing that was an unusual New Zealand politics until recently – apart from John Key. You know, a man with no political background, until then a passive member of the National party, wealthy, handsome and articulate, who suddenly stands for office in some high-level capacity. And of course, with the regulation pretty wife and three children. Sorry, if the sarcasm offends you, but I'm very suspicious of this guy.'

She paused to think for a moment, to recall other things that stood out about Gerald Miller. 'And he's very vocal about his "inclusive" goals for Auckland Council and his admiration for women in business – he's ideal candidate material, something for everyone. And with some strategically mentioned views on how we could change the way immigrants are screened for example, which will make him popular with a certain section of the voters. He hasn't said it yet, but what he probably means is restricting people of colour unless they have higher educations or specialities that we need and then restricting access further by degrees – stealth racism.'

She stopped and looked at Ben, who probably felt she was making huge leaps of assumptions, but he looked back and said nothing, so she continued. 'I've read just about every word Miller has published or said in public. I made it my mission to find out what he really stands for because of possible links to … but I'll revert to that shortly. So, the letter from Gerald Miller's grandfather, who had the same name as the current guy, and who was Gerhart to his friend Hermann, was written forty-one years after these two men arrived in New Zealand in 1950, when they both spoke what was accepted as UK English, possibly explained as some regional accent in their fake life histories, so nobody questioned their identities — but I'll get back to that later too.'

'And what you found out led to your dismissal?'

'Yes, but I must back-track a bit here. The letter was written in English, which might seem surprising if you believe my theory, but I think probably these guys were so used to writing and speaking English after forty years here that it had become normal. I know this seems off when you consider Hermann writing his original German name in that book, but then aren't we all a bit random at times? I think both these men, who arrived on a ship from South America, were either former Nazi officers, or maybe they had managed a concentration camp or something similar, perhaps a forced labour camp in some industry that supplied the army. I haven't gone down that track yet. I chose to concentrate on the grandson first, the man who is now hoping to be the mayor of our biggest city. Sorry, I've got to pee, back in a moment.'

'Hey, I forgot to say,' said Ben when she returned, 'there's another toilet on the far side of the kitchen, off the laundry. So don't feel you're stuck if I'm in the bathroom.'

He gestured at the bottle of red wine and the two glasses that had appeared on the table while Emma was absent. 'Would you like a glass of wine? I think half past four is OK to have a glass under special circumstances. I never drink in the day and never on my own, so today is a great opportunity to have a glass.'

'I'd love it, yes please. Why do you have rules about drinking? Is it all those empty calories, thinking of your figure?'

'No, I'm not worried about that – or not yet, and I do have a beer now and then even when I'm here alone, but I think I might have an addictive personality, so I limit various things to make sure I stay safe. And no, please don't look like that, there's no need to reassess my character. I never did get addicted to anything, but I just have a feeling about it. I don't watch or read porn either, like the majority of single men seem to do – and many others. I just stay away from the lot.' He chuckled. 'They call me the Puritan at the station. They probably laugh about me behind my back, discuss how crazy I am.'

He's fascinating, thought Emma and looked at the serious face looking back at her. He's probably unique, I really like him. I don't think I've ever met anyone like him before, well, I'm sure I haven't, he's so cool. And the way his smile makes me feel warm, it's very strange.

'Well?' said Ben. 'Let's leave my puritanism to one side. I'd like to hear how you worked it all out?'

'I'll give you the letter to read, it's in that Latin grammar book-box for safekeeping. And I have photos of the letter and the envelope on my phone. Did I say the letter was written in 1991? It describes in detail and with much satisfaction how Gerhart/Gerald was busy indoctrinating his grandson and namesake, then aged twelve, with his own ideology, making him proud of secretly being a little neo-Nazi, and outlining how he planned to introduce him in his teens to an organisation which he only refers to as the "Brotherhood" – with a capital B. Which I suspect is a right-wing, white supremacist group. Do you see it now?'

'Shit, yes! *Please* tell me you didn't put this stuff on social media! Were those guys at the river part of this Brotherhood, do you think?'

'Oh, yes – and they made no secret of it, they made sure I knew. They told me what would happen to me if I revealed anything in public. And the only comfort I have now, is that they have no idea about who it was I was overheard talking to about this. I know I haven't got to that bit yet, but I will. That's how this started, my dismissal, the threats at the river – it all comes back to me being stupid and talking about the letter in a public place. The person, who overheard must have recognised me, probably from the library. I know it's a tangled tale, but it all hangs together once you line up the facts.'

During another long silence from Ben, Emma

suddenly felt depleted, desperately tired, nearly dizzy. She put her nearly untouched glass on the table, slid down on the sofa, put a cushion under her head and closed her eyes. A few moments later she said without opening her eyes, 'But Nadine is safe, she's not from here – nobody knows her. Sorry, I can't keep my eyes open.'

Emma slept deeply for a couple of hours, unaware of Ben pulling curtains and turning lights on, preparing dinner and lighting a fire in the living room fireplace. She didn't know that he kept coming back to stand beside the sofa looking down at her, or the conflicting thoughts that went through his mind as he worked around her. She didn't hear him check the front door and put the safety chain on, and she didn't see him use his phone to set the external camera and lights to come on if someone approached the house.

But she woke up when he was standing by the fire with a glass of wine in his hand, absently staring at the flames and said something out loud to himself, and she sat up confused and disorientated. 'What? What did you say?'

She didn't know that he lied when he said he was only telling himself he must wake her up for dinner, instead of confessing what he had said to himself: 'I hope to God they have no idea she's here'.

· · · ·

They had another glass of wine over dinner of vegetable lasagne from the deli on High Street, which Emma was familiar with from her previous life, as she called it whenever she reflected on how her life had changed. Halfway through her helping, Emma, still tired and with the wineglass tilting in her hand, looked dreamily down at the plate in front of her and said quietly, 'This, my friend, is like heaven. A glass of wine and a hot meal, a proper dinner. I am so grateful for all this.'

Ben smiled and lifted his glass in a silent toast, then returned to the conversation they had started before dinner, before she fell asleep on the sofa. 'Tell me about that café, what happened there and who were you talking to?'

'My friend Nadine, who lives in Cambridge, was on a long road trip all around the South Island visiting relations and friends, and one day she texted and said she'd be in town the next day, and could we have lunch somewhere nice. So, we met at the French Bistro – you know the one by the park - and got a booth by the window. Well, they're not booths really, but there's a head high partition between the tables along the side wall, head high when you're sitting down, I mean. We've just reconnected after a little incident in our last year of library studies, and though I hadn't seen her for a decade, I do trust her. I thought telling her the whole story would be like a test. If she thought my theory was nonsense, she'd tell me, and I'd take note of her opinion, she's *very* sensible and grounded.'

She took another mouthful of lasagne and continued as soon as she had swallowed. 'So, we got the table next to the window, and I checked that the table next to us behind the little partition was empty, and then I started telling her the story and showed her the photos of the letter and the envelope I have on my phone.'

Emma took a sip of wine and shook her head at her own negligence. 'I was so careless - I wasn't alert enough. She was sitting with her back to the partition, and I had my back to the window, but then I realised there must be someone there, because a waitress was coming across with a plate in her hand. I put my fingers across my lips to stop Nadine from continuing what she was saying, and we left immediately.'

'Ah!' said Ben. 'Lucky that he – or she - didn't get photos of you on your way out.'

'Well, as soon as I realised the implications, that whoever was sitting there must have heard at least part of the conversation, I took my phone out of her hand and typed a text message saying that she should go outside and wait while I paid, and to try to keep her face turned away on the way out, so that guy wouldn't get a look at her. I'd put my finger over my lips to stop her talking the moment I realised he was there. And I passed the phone over so she could read what I'd typed, but I didn't send it.' She drank some of her wine and took another mouthful of food before she continued. 'I realised that if I couldn't establish a link between the current Miller and the Brotherhood or something similar, then nothing in the letter mattered, but what I was telling Nadine could get me sued for slander – that was the concern I had. At that time, I didn't know if the Brotherhood still existed.'

'Apart from what those guys at the river said, have you found any evidence that the Brotherhood still exists?'

'No, nothing. But to get back to the slander worry - according to what I've read online, Miller is quite keen on suing people, he's done it multiple time. In one article he was quoted as saying "it's a useful mechanism to make the public aware". Not that I completely understand what he means, but that's what he said.'

She paused and thought for a moment, trying to sum up what else it was that had alarmed her in the café. 'Oh, and if I *did* manage to establish a link to any of today's neo-Nazi organisations, then I had an unexploded bomb on my hands, of course. Until those guys down by the river mentioned the Brotherhood and how they knew I had talked to someone about this, I hadn't established the direct link.'

Emma twirled the stem of her wine glass between her fingers, lost in thought for a few moments. 'Let's say those two German's were implicated in war crimes or something similar, then all their descendants here would be affected if it came out. This isn't just about

Miller junior. It seems like an issue fraught with complications, quite apart from the impact of having a mayor with Nazi leanings and associations with far-right groups that the public wouldn't know about.'

"Your instincts are excellent,' said Ben. 'You'd make a good detective. I assume that whoever overheard that conversation in the bistro told someone else, but who? Have you worked it out?'

'I'll go back a bit, and it will become clear. The guys at the river said I had to stop talking about it, and the only person I have talked to in a public place, where I might have been overheard, was Nadine. I did tell a colleague from the library, but apart from one brief comment in the staff room at work, I told her in private. And my face is familiar, anyone who uses the library might recognise me. The staff at the bistro know me, one of them sometimes mentions a book she's reading, so if the person at the table next to us asked who I was, they'd easily find out that I worked at the library.'

Emma scraped the last of the lasagne off the plate, making sure she left nothing behind, and caught a strange look on Ben's face, maybe pity, and felt confused. Pity? Why? She dismissed the thought and answered his question.

'So, I imagine it went like this, just a theory. That person in the bistro knows the mayor here or maybe works for him, or knows that our mayor is friends with the Miller guy in Auckland — or possibly the listener himself knows Miller? Or they belong the that damn group of neo-Nazis – or it could be seven steps down the line, who knows? Anyway, if Miller was told about me by someone here, it could explain why I got made redundant for a false reason - the library is a city council facility, so maybe someone higher up the food chain at the council said, get rid of Emma on some pretext. And then Miller *or* the local mayor, or whoever, contacted the local chapter of the Brotherhood and told them to deal with me, to shut me up. Something like that – it's impossible to work out. There are lots of potential connections and I have no way of proving exactly how it happened, but I'm certain it did.'

There was silence for a moment. Emma watched Ben's forehead crease as he stared into empty space and considered all the possibilities she had listed, and then she remembered that she had left out a crucial bit and said, 'Hey, I didn't say *how* I know the redundancy was fake,' and told him about Anne overhearing Cora's phone conversation.

After another pause, Ben said, 'I think you're most likely right.' He reached over to take her plate. 'It's roughly what I'd put together as a potential explanation too, just an outline, when you said someone overheard you talking in a public place – but of course, I didn't come up with any detail, just a sketchy explanation. There's got to be a connection. And it doesn't matter exactly how these things join up, the fact is that somehow they do.' He got to his feet and took their plates over to the kitchen bench.

'And here's another little snippet – not directly linked, but interesting,' said Emma. 'My friend Fletcher has lived here for some years, much longer than I have, but we've always stayed in touch, ever since high school. He was one of the reasons I moved here after … after a tragedy a couple of years ago. Fletcher said, come and live here, it's a nice city, lots of great things to do and you need a complete change of scene where you have no history.'

Realising she was getting side-tracked and was on the verge of revealing personal things she would rather not discuss, she stopped and thought for a moment before she continued. 'Anyway, he's the manager of Mountain View Lodge outside town, that high-end place where wealthy people stay. He knows absolutely everyone worth knowing here, all the people with influence and/or money. They go out there for drinks and private birthday parties or weddings, all kinds of things. He overheard a conversation in that grand foyer they have at the lodge. Have you been there?'

'Only once,' said Ben. 'It's not really my kind of place, but I must admit that huge foyer with the big stone fireplace is fantastic. Have *you* been?'

Emma laughed and shook her head. 'God no, it's way out of my league, but I've seen photos and a lovely video, and Fletcher has promised to have me for dinner in the restaurant there for my next birthday. He's disgusted about me getting sacked. Apart from Fletcher and Anne, she's the one who told me about that phone call, and Nadine, I've told nobody about this until today.'

'So, this means that aside from yourself, only four people know about your research?'

Emma counted in her head: Anne, Fletcher, Nadine and Ben, then she nodded. 'Yep, four plus me.'

'Quite a complicated story,' said Ben from the kitchen bench. 'Let's tidy up and go and sit in the living room again, so we can discuss this a bit further.'

Chapter 18

Back in the living room after tidying up the in the kitchen, Ben surprised her. 'I'd like to know what your surname is. I know there are things you don't want to talk about, but surely your surname isn't one of them?'

'Of course not! I just hadn't realised you don't know it already. My full name is Emma Louise Stewart, I was born in Tauranga where my mother still lives with my stepfather David. I'm thirty-four years old. My younger brother Arch is hoping to become a professional surfer and could be anywhere at any time, we never know until we get a message, usually asking for money. My dad runs a charter boat for divers in Queensland. And that's about it, full disclosure. But ask anything – I have no reservations about you now, that was just at the start when I thought you'd go into full detective-mode if I told you the story.'

'You can trust me, I promise - you know that. Or I hope you do. And now that I've heard it all, I think making this official would definitely put you at risk. Those extremist groups can be relentless and might think nothing of taking the law into their own hands. But I'll make some discrete enquiries at the station without mentioning you at all. If you don't mind.'

Instantly her sense of threat ramped up. 'What kind of enquiries?'

He didn't reply to her question, instead he said, 'I'm thinking of their car too, if you can remember any details. You said they drove in just after you, so you saw it. What kind of car was it?'

Emma cast her mind back, pictured the scene and tried to focus on the vehicle and after a while she said, 'I think if I tell you how it played out, like step by step, more detail might come back to me. I've been going over what happened in my mind, but I kind of miss the car, it's just a car, nothing specific − well, it's a black SUV, but that's all.'

'Do that and take as long as you like.' He sat back and waited, and she thought again how unusual his approach was, the way he just waited in silence, didn't feel a need to fill the gap with comments, wasn't tempted to change the subject or fidget. He just sat there and waited, sturdy and patient. She wondered what was going through his mind, was he thinking of something else entirely, or was he working on what he already knew, piecing things together?

She pulled her own thoughts together and said, 'This is how it was – I decided to go to that place, which I've seen from the main road, where you kind of look down on it from higher up, but I'd never stopped there before. It was prompted by someone I know who posted photos of it on Facebook and Instagram, saying how much she longed for summer. So off I went thinking I'd be a couple of hours – I just wanted to get away from that chilly container, that locked-in feeling of always being in a small space. When I saw the sign to the rocks there was a black SUV right behind me, so I pulled over to the side and let it pass before I crossed to the access road. There was one car there, just about to leave.'

A pause while she considered how much detail to include, but she decided she had to tell him everything, if the process of jogging her memory was going to work. 'First I walked upstream to the big boulders and took some photos, but the water was so deep and fast flowing I couldn't get out to them. And now that I think about it – there must be a ladder lying around somewhere out there, or how to people get up on the biggest rock? Anyway, I walked back downstream to where there's a swimming hole. Did you know about it before last night?'

'Yes, I've been there several times with Ari's kids.'

'Well, I stood there for a couple of minutes, thinking how weird it was that the river flowed past that bay so fast, but the water in the bay itself was nearly still. I was standing there watching a big fish that was kind of suspended in the water and admiring how the light on its back made it glisten. And then I heard a car coming down off the main road and doors slamming, so I turned to look. It was a black SUV, and two guys got out and came towards me.'

She frowned and looked into the middle distance without focus for a moment, tried to force her mind to see the car more clearly. 'I don't know the make - I was looking at those men and thinking that maybe being there on my own wasn't a very good idea, after all.'

She shook off the feeling the remembered scene had generated and continued. 'It was the way they came directly towards me that made me a bit apprehensive, they were so … focused, as if they were on a mission and I was the target. They came right up to me where I was standing looking at that fish, and then they split up a step or two before they reached me, and one went around behind me, so I was kind of hemmed in.'

She could hear her voice becoming tense and made an effort to sound calm, to lower the pitch. 'One took hold of my arm and the other one said I had two choices. I could give up the book and the letter and never mention them to anyone ever again and they'd let me go. Oh, *and* I must give them my phone. Or they would break me – that's what they said, they would break me.'

The feeling of threat seemed to be in the room with

her now, she felt her heartbeats speed up and stopped talking. Ben looked carefully at her and said, 'Can you describe them?' His question calmed her, made her feel safer, as if sticking to facts was a remedy for the fear she was starting to re-live by telling the story.

'They were probably in their early or mid-thirties, white, quite fit-looking. Very normal looking, too, nothing extreme. They were in jeans, one had only a white T-shirt on and the other a sweatshirt, brownish hair, very short haircuts. If I had met them anywhere else I wouldn't have felt alarmed for a second.'

She tried to remember any other details that might help to identify them. 'And well-spoken, as my mum would say. Not rough - well, *what* they said was rough but not *how* they said it, it was like we were having a casual conversation. Perhaps it felt worse, more frightening, because they sounded so calm, so normal, as if talking about brutality was a casual thing for them. One had a tattoo on the upside of his right wrist, I saw it when I wrenched his hand off my arm and he tried to grab my hand. An eagle like those ones you see on official insignia, spread out wings, clawed feet forward – impressive.'

She paused, mentally summed up what she had told him and added, 'The detail of the threat – that's what put me into panic mode. I wouldn't have had a chance against the two of them.'

Ben's focus on her was so intense it felt like sunburn on her face. 'What did they say they would do to you?'

'They would break my arms and legs one at a time and ...' She took a deep breath. 'And then they would throw me in the river. Which was, of course, the same thing as saying they would do terrible, painful things to me and then watch me drown. So, I jumped into that deep pool and swam across it into the flow of the river itself and ...'

But saying it, however factually and calmly, made her tremble. She felt the terror she had experienced at the time, how her wet clothes threatened to drag her down, how her heart felt as if it would stop at the shock of the freezing water. Now her breath caught in her throat, she was choking, and she leapt to her feet with her fists clenched and stood there without knowing where to go, gripped by an urge to flee.

Ben was by her side before she even noticed he had got up, took hold of her upper arms and said, 'It's OK, Emma - you're safe here. Take deep breaths, slow, deep breaths. I won't let anything happen to you.'

The feeling that those warm hands on her arms gave her, the way he sounded so steady, so reliable, broke through the fear. Instinctively she leaned her forehead against his shoulder, and he pulled her closer, both hands on her back. Neither of them said anything for what seemed like minutes, then he dropped his hands and said, 'OK now? Do you want to go to bed?'

She choked back a gurgle of laughter, surprising herself as much as it probably surprised him. 'Are you completely *mad*? Go to bed *now*? When I've not even finished the story? Don't you want to hear what else I've just remembered?'

In her head this sudden panic and then calming down, the feeling that her fear and what had happened to her was known by somebody else, and that she was safe, had for some strange reason unlocked a memory.

He chuckled and said mockingly, as if he was quoting a line in a book, 'And suddenly she turned into Superwoman, and left him standing there feeling like a fool.'

'Wow!' she said, sat down again and started to laugh. 'That was amazing — do you come up with things like that in your job? To lighten the mood, maybe?'

'Shit no! I'd never say a thing like that on the job! But I often find random phrases popping into my head. I only say things like that in front of Ari and the kids, and it makes them laugh, but I'd never even do it in front of my three older brothers, they'd think I'd gone mad.'

'I love it, it's funny and clever, very clever. But, seriously, I've just remembered the number plate on that SUV – PRU357.'

He paused in the act of sitting down with an arrested look on his face and stared at her. 'What? You remember the whole plate? Just like that?'

'Let me explain,' she replied and tried to make it sound reasonable that she could do this. 'Prue is a friend of mine from when I lived in Taupo, 3 and 5 and 7 are the first three prime numbers. I often kind of subconsciously register patterns or sequences in numbers, like phone numbers or number plates. You know, as if they're in code and my mind tries to decipher them. It must have stored it away when I glanced at the car, before those guys had my full attention, which of course distracted me. And then I was in the river and never saw the car again.'

'Isn't number one a prime number?'

'Do you want the full lecture or the short version?' asked Emma and Ben said, 'Short version, please.'

She said calmly, 'One isn't a proper prime number because I say so.'

His forehead creased. 'What? Is that the short version?'

'Just a silly joke. My mum used to say it, so either we did what she wanted, just because she said so, or else we got a long and tedious explanation why something needed to be done – about how helping each other is what people do in a family, and on, and on, and on! So, naturally we always chose the short version and just went and did whatever it was she wanted us to do.'

'Can I have the full lecture, then? Because now I really want to know.'

'A prime number has two qualifiers – one is that it can be divided only by itself or by the number 1, which is the same thing really. The second qualifier is that it can be divided by *another* number and the result must be a full number, no fractions. But when you check those rules against the number1, you'll find that there is really only one qualifier. Or you could say that one qualifier does both jobs.'

She sat quietly studying his face as he thought about this with creases between his eyebrows and his gaze unfocused. And she thought how strange it seemed that she already knew how typical this was. No questions, no thinking out loud while he worked it out, just silently thinking. I really like it, she thought, he's very restful to be with. Now, how many people would have asked her about number 1 not being a true prime number, in the first place? Another unusual thing.

'OK, it seems like a kind of circular argument,' he said finally, 'but it makes sense. So, some people regard it as a prime?'

'Oh, yes – it is a prime, but it's often described as "not a *true* prime" and I kind of like the distinction.'

'Finish your wine,' said Ben and got to his feet. 'I'll put some more wood on the fire and then we'll continue. I really want to hear the end of this saga so we can start figuring out what to do next.'

He threw a couple of pieces of wood into the fire and returned to his armchair. 'And talk about amazing! You're full of surprises. But can we back up a bit? You know how you said those two men who arrived on a ship from South America spoke such good English and had UK passports. How did you know where to dig up facts like that?'

'Some of it from the *Paperspast* website,' she said. 'They've got the New Zealand newspapers digitised now from way back in the eighteen hundreds to the end of the nineteen-fifties, so I just searched by names. It didn't take long – I just searched a couple of years in case that arrival year in the recent newspaper article from when Gerald Miller senior died, was wrong by a year or two. And then it was just a question of finding the highlighted name Gerald Miller wherever it cropped up and checking it referred to the right person. It appeared in a Dominion article from nineteen-fifty about recent new arrivals.'

'Can you find it again?'

'I bookmarked it on my laptop, and I've also got screenshots of the article on my hard drive. Why?'

Ben stretched and instead of replying or returning to his chair, he remained standing by the fire. 'Let's have some ice cream – do you like ice cream?'

Emma laughed again, because this man was so intriguing and so amusing that it made her feel happy and relaxed in a way she hadn't experienced for a long time.

'Of course, I like ice cream – provided it's not one of those with crushed biscuits mixed in - or caramel. I hope it's the maple syrup and walnut kind, it's my favourite.'

'Come with me,' said Ben and she followed him to

the kitchen where he opened the freezer and pulled out a drawer. 'Your choice.'

She stared at the drawer, which contained at least five boxes of different ice creams alongside a large bag of frozen minted peas. 'Wow! I don't think I've ever known anyone who had so much ice cream in the house!'

'Ah,' he said smugly. 'The things you can do when you live on your own, eh? Lots of kinds of ice cream to eat any time of the night and day, peas with everything, alternating coffee and tea without causing confusion – endless egotistical pleasures.'

They returned to the living room with bowls of ice cream, and Emma recalled the unfinished story about the article she had found on the Paperspast website and started again.

'That old newspaper article was probably written because one of the passengers was a famous Argentinian writer, who was coming here for a lecture and book launch tour. The reporter was at the arrival place on the wharf, whatever it was called, where they checked passports and papers. And perhaps on impulse, he grabbed another few arrivals and wrote up their stories as a separate article, just short profiles. Those two Germans weren't the only ones, he interviewed four others too. Once I'd found them and knew the date they arrived, I kept looking for a period forward, but I found nothing else that linked to them in the next couple of years.'

She ate some more maple syrup and walnut ice cream and said, 'What an amazing evening this has been, Ben. A hot meal and lovely wine, remembering that number plate, an anxiety attack fixed by a very calm man, who makes up entertaining random quotes, and five choices of ice cream to eat late at night. Can I stay here forever?'

And then she realised how that flippant question could be taken and felt her face go red with embarrassment. 'Oh God, I'm sorry - I'm only joking, please don't panic!'

Ben said, calm as always and with no particular emphasis, 'I think you should – stay forever, I mean.'

And as Emma sat looking down at her hands without being able to think of any kind of response, he continued as if he hadn't just said something extraordinary, 'But finish telling me about that article because I might have just thought of the perfect way to make things safe for you again without concealing information the public should know before the elections. Provided we can demonstrate a credible link between Miller and those Brotherhood thugs, of course - we don't want to defame the man if they're nothing to do with him. If my idea works, it would be a way of defusing this situation without involving you at all, make it seem like a coincidence - as if someone else came across the same information and made it public.'

'Great! Are you going to work tomorrow?' She tried to sound casual and calm, while inside her head his words "I think you should stay forever" played on an endless loop, disturbing and exciting in equal parts.

'I don't go back until next week, so we have plenty of time. Why?'

'Tomorrow morning I'd like to show you *everything* I have, The book and the letter, the article on that website and anything else I came up with. I did so much searching, I researched every aspect I could think of. The only mystery is who those two Germans were before they went to Argentina, but I might do that next, after this is over. I found several mentions of how the Nazis, who fled to South American countries, had all kinds of things set up in readiness before the war ended, when they knew they were losing. Like places to go, language coaches, people who could produce false passports and identities, and whole fake life stories. All kinds of things that were so much easier then - before everything could be checked on the internet. I'll find it all again and show you.'

Lying in bed in that nearly empty bedroom Emma realised that simply being in the same house as another human being, even with her bedroom door closed, as Ben's presumably was too, made her feel like a different person from the one who lived in the container. As if just another presence had pulled her back into the normal main-stream of life and restored her to the real world, no longer left behind. Going back to the container will be hard, very hard, she thought, but I'll have this interlude in this lovely place and how I felt here to think about.

Chapter 19

Over breakfast of tea and toast, she got the perfect opportunity to ask something she had wondered about but hadn't been able to think of a way to bring up until now. She turned down the offer of a second slice of toast, but he simply put it on her plate anyway and repeated what he said the previous day, 'You've lost weight lately, I think. Have another slice of toast, it will do you good.'

'You sound like my mother,' said Emma and reached for the butter. 'Well, not quite the same, *she* would give me a whole little lecture, and then she'd bring it up again three times today. But I'm just naturally quite slim, so losing weight happens fast. *Why* do you think I've lost weight? We hadn't met before you picked me up on the road.'

'Don't forget I pulled your damp jeans off you, and they seemed lose at the waist, which was odd because wet clothes usually seem to tighten on the body as they begin to dry and be difficult to get off. So, I thought you might not have been quite so thin a while ago.'

At first, she hesitated to comment on this astute observation, but he did already know her situation, so she said, 'OK, you're right, I've lost a bit of weight because I can't cook properly in the container, so I just heat up simple thing, and it's often not what I feel like eating. And sometimes I don't have a proper meal or even a halfway proper meal, I just don't feel like it. I can't afford to buy those nice pre-cooked or frozen meals more than once a week or so. Sometimes I have cheese on a slice of toast, which makes a nice meal, but usually I just have soup.'

'Toast with cheese is great,' he said and pulled the jar of jam towards him. 'But if you don't have proper meals you soon lose weight.'

'I'm aware of it, but my mood's been … bleak. I often can't be bothered eating.'

'And no friends locally who could let you use their shower, feed you a decent meal? And now I think of it, you don't have a toilet either. How do you cope?'

'The visitors' centre downtown has showers you can use for a few dollars, and you get long enough to get clean and wash your hair, so I go there two or three times a week. And I do have a toilet − well, it's an old-fashioned long-drop, a hole in the ground inside a little shed, very cold.'

She hesitated for a moment before she told him

something she found disturbing to even think about when she was alone, when she sometimes wondered if she had become slightly unbalanced by what her life had turned into.

'I've not wanted to tell people how my life has fallen apart. Even though it isn't my fault, I feel so humiliated to be in a situation like this. I've not been in the right mood to cope with pity or lots of sympathy, so I've just concealed it and stopped meeting people in places I can't afford. Even Fletcher and my mother know nothing about the container. They think I've moved to a studio flat behind someone's house.'

She gave him a wry smile. 'I've become a master of evasion and deceit. I can dream up an excuse for not meeting someone in a wine bar or for lunch in two seconds flat. I was hoping I'd find a job, but it's hard for a trained librarian to get other jobs. People look at your CV and say you're over-qualified, and that's apparently as bad as having no skills at all in the eyes of most employers.'

'I've heard that before, more than once. Have you not had a job at all since they forced you out?'

'I washed dishes in a restaurant for a few weeks for the minimum pay, and I would have continued, but then I got dermatitis from the detergent and the hot water, and it only got worse if I wore gloves. The heat and sweat inside the gloves, I think.'

'You haven't applied for the benefit?'

'No, I'm just getting to the stage now when I'm

thinking of doing that, because I realise that however much I don't want to, before long I'll have to or I'll starve if I don't get a job.'

'Are you living on your savings? I know you said giving up the nice flat was a saving and so is the terrible diet, but how much longer can you live on savings?'

'I sold my good car and bought that terrible wreck you saw - that's my so-called savings fund. If I'm careful I can live on that for months and it gives me time to get another proper job or move.'

'And then you'd have to start all over again, saving up for a better car, finding a flat and all the rest?'

'Yes.'

Telling this sad tale to someone for the first time was both liberating and hard. She had kept up the pretence of being all right with her mother and managed to avoid telling outright lies by manipulating conversations to fit. Fletcher had no idea, because they had always met on a Monday or Tuesday at lunchtime, so there was nothing different about it now, and those she met for coffee still knew nothing. Thinking back on it now, it seemed incredible that she had kept up the pretence of normal life for so long and with so many. Did it say something about her or about them? Was she unexpectedly good at lying, or were they not observant enough?

Ben got up and walked behind her, bent to pick up her mug and put his hand on her shoulder. 'You're an amazing girl, but I think you've isolated yourself too much. Not to mention what a bad idea it was to not apply for the benefit right away.'

She looked down at the table and said nothing, and he continued, as if he hadn't expected an answer. 'Time someone looked after you a bit, I think, this obviously can't continue. Coffee, or more tea?'

'Oh, yes please, I'd love a coffee,' she said, feeling shy suddenly and slightly uncertain. Did he think of her as a child, who needed looking after, despite the fact that he was probably only six or eight years older? She hesitated to even admit to herself how much she liked him and how she found him increasingly attractive, very attractive. He might well have a girlfriend, she thought, or someone he's got his eye on. I mustn't get carried away and start imagining things.

Ben swept a few last crumbs off the table into his hand. 'Now then,' he said. 'I put your washing that was in the bucket in the machine last night and I tossed it in the dryer before breakfast, so do you want to get it out first? Before we start this, I mean. I heard the dryer beep a few minutes ago.'

'You did what?' she said and felt her face go red with embarrassment. 'You did my laundry?'

'What's wrong? Are you upset about it?' He looked carefully at her, puzzled by her exclamation.

'I ...' she hesitated and started again. 'I'm sorry, it's

very kind of you to do that, but I was taken by surprise. I'm a bit odd about things like that.'

'What things? Washing? Dryers?'

She knew she had to tell him, and she couldn't look at him when she said, very fast, 'It's ridiculous, I know that, but I felt embarrassed at the thought of you putting my panties in the machine.'

He burst out laughing and said in his quoting voice, 'They were the perfect match, the Puritan and the Prude, and lived happily ever after.'

And she laughed too, ignored the dryer, and said, 'Let's start working right away.'

'Go and get your laptop and stuff, and we'll sit here and look at all the things you found. I'll bring mine too, so we can work together – maybe I can do things to save time,' he said when they had put things away after breakfast.

Emma had to make two trips from her room to bring the laptop and the chargers, her blue notebook, a pen, the fake Latin grammar and her phone. While she organised her things around her, Ben plugged in both their laptops and his phone to charge in a multi-socket power board.

'Last night you said you thought you knew how to defuse this mess,' she said and started flicking pages in her notebook, searching through all the notes she had made when she started looking for clues about the letter. 'Are you going to tell me?'

'Of course.'

He reached for her phone charger and plugged it into the last socket. 'Where's your phone?'

She handed it to him and wondered if he was deliberately stalling, if he would now say it must become a police matter, and what she could say or do if that was the case. It felt as if her presence here had suddenly become temporary and uncertain, and she said nothing as he sat down opposite her and turned his laptop on.

'Ari's daughter Kiri is one of those tech orientated kids who seem to know incredible things about what can be done on the internet. She actually understands how it works, quite advanced things, and she can explain it all in minute detail – which she does and which I pretend to understand and then promptly forget. I sent her a text before she went to school and asked her if she could do what I felt we need, and she said yes, easy-peasy, she can do it.'

'Which is what?'

'Look at it like this,' he said, serious now. 'We've got to keep both of us invisible, but this story must be told, if we find that it links Miller to the Brotherhood. So that's the first thing I want Kiri to do, and she'll do it on something called a VPN address that means she can't be identified - I think.' He paused and looked out the window with a frown. 'Now that I think about it, she has all the makings of an IT criminal, hasn't she? I'll have to keep an eye on her. But anyway, in some untraceable way she'll try to find out more about this group called the Brotherhood and see if she can find any references to Gerald Miller, and then we'll go from there.'

'Where will we go?'

'You and I – mainly you, will compile a complete file of every single thing you've found, including any reasonable assumptions. When that's as complete as it can be, including scans of the book, the envelope and the letter, we'll put it on a USB stick. I said I'd email it to Kiri, and she said - hang on a minute and I'll read it out, so I get it right.'

He picked up his phone, checked his text messages and said: 'Cos you cant email dangerous stuff blockhead not safe. Put it on a usb i'll pick it up if u say when.'

He handed her his phone across the table so she could see for herself and laughed. 'No commas, one full stop and only capitals where the system put them in automatically. But she's super smart so we'll do what she says and put it on a USB stick. A fourteen-year-old little wizard.'

'You still haven't told me what the plan is, Ben!'

'Patience, girl! I'm coming to it. Then she'll contact those organisations that dig and find out if candidates standing in the local elections have hidden agendas and make them public - and she'll somehow safely and anonymously send them the info we give her. No names, no trace to follow that could lead back to you or me. And don't ask me how she does that, because it might be better that we don't know.'

'You also said you'd find some stuff out from work, meaning police, so what's that about?'

'Oh, just asking around if anyone knows which local candidates in the elections are nutters, the ones who spread disinformation and conspiracy nonsense. I'll just say I'm keen not to vote for any of them by mistake. The election's only a couple of months away and there's been a bit of discussion about this already at work. We've got a few who've disappeared down the conspiracy rabbit hole, so it might turn into a heated debate again, but I think you'd find one or two of those in nearly any workplace these days.'

The next couple of hours was a demonstration of cooperation in the face of nearly irreconcilable differences of opinion. It started well with discussions about how to present the material to make it easy to follow, to present it in a way that pulled facts and assumptions into a coherent story. After various ideas had been discarded, Emma suggested using bullet points as a format for the entire story.

'Calling it a story minimises it,' said Ben. 'Makes it sound like we made it up. Let's call it report and make it sound official and formal. So, what's the bullet point format going to look like?'

'We have main points numbered, so number one

would be the letter, then sub-points with various explanations and assumptions that stemmed from the main point.'

'No way! We can't make the letter number one or any number at all. If one of those organisations we're sending the report to mentions the letter, you're in the spotlight again. They must be persuaded to publish what we tell them, as if it's come to light some other way, so we have to be creative. The whole point of my plan is to remove any suspicion that the leak originated with you.'

'But the letter is the *proof* of the original assumption, the only proof,' protested Emma. 'How else can it be explained? How else would the German link come into it? It's the only thing that mentions their original names. Anything else would seem unsubstantial, not definitive enough and nobody would believe it.'

'No need to explain anything, I don't think,' said Ben. 'Just collate all the evidence, make the people we send it to draw their own conclusion and make their own assumptions. Let's suggest that there have been rumours about Miller's grandfather for years, and that those rumours link him to that guy who owned the maths book – but we don't mention the book, just the man. And somehow or other we introduce the fact that it's been whispered that Miller, the present-day version, has been involved with neo-Nazis since his early teenage years.'

'We can't! How *could* you suggest that — you're a police officer for God's sake. We don't know that for fact, the whole thing might be local and have nothing to do with him, as I told you at the start! And I don't think anyone would dare publish it without the letter and the book as evidence.'

They sat at the table with their laptops, not just physically opposite each other, but on different sides in an increasingly frustrating debate.

'We need to compromise, or we'll have to come up with a completely different solution,' said Ben. 'And I can see you aren't prepared to compromise. And here I was, prepared to act untruthfully and conceal evidence to protect you!' He gave her a wry smile across the table. 'But I think you're right — I let my protective instinct take over and beat down common sense. So where to from here?'

'I'm very grateful that you want to protect me,' said Emma. 'It makes me feel very special and safe. But let's have a break and go and look at your garden, I really want to see it. I've seen the back garden through the windows, and it looks amazing. Can we?'

'Anything you like,' said Ben. 'Just put your jacket on, there's often a deceptively cold wind up here on this slope in winter. The sun shines and it looks great, and then you go out and you freeze in minutes.'

Chapter 20

Emma stopped on the step outside the back door and smiled at Ben who had come out ahead of her while she got her jacket, ignoring his own jacket or the chilly little wind off the snow.

'And Superman headed out into the arctic cold without his jacket and ignored the icicles in his beard,' she said mockingly. 'Doesn't cold affect you?'

'Let's get this clear,' he replied. 'Body mass protects you, it's insulation. I have lots and you have hardly any. Good thing we've got all that ice cream and chocolate in the house. I'm not letting you get chilled so soon after nearly dying from hypothermia, but I'm not at risk. And also, in case you hadn't noticed, I don't have a beard.'

'OK,' said Emma meekly but inwardly laughing, and followed him down the path towards the steep slope at the end of the garden. 'Was all this here when you bought the house?'

'Some of it was. Not those terraced vegetable gardens, that was just a grass slope with some boring trees, nothing productive.' He pointed to the left. 'That part of the flat area was covered in half a ton of white gravel with a huge blue urn thing sitting in the middle – they took the urn, thank God. The gravel area had collected all the dead leaves and debris known to man, so I cleared it out and gave it to a friend, nine very heavy wheelbarrow loads – gravel weighs a lot. Lawn is much easier to look after, and the vegetable beds are quite enough work and they're productive which makes them worthwhile.'

Emma went slowly up the steps that led from one terraced growing bed to the next with narrow tracks on the uphill side of each bed to walk on to pick things in summer. Now the only vegetables were winter ones, and the empty beds were covered in mulch. But she could picture how easy it would be to plant and harvest from those bed. Stand on the path on the level below and there's the patch you're working on at thigh level, she thought, so practical and attractive to look at too.

'Like those terraced hillsides in Asia where they grow rice – very clever of you. Lots of work though, terracing that slope must have been backbreaking. You obviously love vegetables.'

'I only like peas, really,' he said, straight faced. 'Which I can't be bothered growing, I buy them frozen.

I give most of the crop away, mostly to Ari, who comes over and helps because she loves this kind of gardening, and they don't have room for a plantation like this one at their place, they live in a townhouse and have a tiny garden, but they're mostly vegetarian. Saves them heaps to get it from here. The kids help too sometimes, particularly Wolf, he's a good little gardener.'

'He's really called Wolf?'

'No, his real name is Adam, but he was always starving as a baby and Ari used to say it was like feeding a wolf, and then the name stuck.'

'I know!' said Emma suddenly. 'I know how we can do it! Let's go back inside and continue compromising.'

'Watch that word!' Ben chuckled. 'Don't get that sentence wrong or you might blush again.'

She looked at him blankly and not until she was hanging her jacket up on the hooks inside the front door did the penny drop, and she laughed. I haven't laughed so much in several months, she thought, as she pulled a brush through her hair, he's such a joy to be with.

'Now then,' said Ben when they were once more sitting opposite each other at the table after lunch. 'Tell me how we can solve this crisis.'

'We give Kiri a lot of single words and names, no context, no assumptions and ask her to use her invisibility cloak on the Internet and search by all those word and names, to see what she comes up with, anything that links to more than one of the search words we gave her. I presume she's on all social media, so she can search there too. And she might find groups that are private, and maybe she can break into them and see what's there? Or articles that mention the names. Unless you think it sounds too dangerous for her.'

He was silent for so long she thought he had forgotten what he was supposed to tell her, but then he looked up.

'I'm having second thoughts about Kiri, I know just the person to do this alongside her,' he said. 'I don't know why I didn't think of him straight off. Ari's brother-in-law is an IT consultant of some kind, and also violently opposed to all this conspiracy shit, those groups that try to destabilise democracy. We were talking about it a few months ago at a barbecue at Ari's place. If he and Kiri work together, he would know how to keep her safe and she would learn heaps, which she'll love. I'll call him before Kiri gets here.'

'Right,' he said when they both felt the list of search words was complete and they had printed it out, having decided that loading it on a USB stick wasn't necessary. 'I'll call Jonty now and see if he'll help us.'

Emma went to the sitting room and tried to look as if she wasn't listening to the conversation she could hear both sides of, because Ben had the phone on speaker and was doing something in the kitchen while he talked.

'Hi,' he said briskly. 'I need a bit of IT security

advice - are you free tonight or tomorrow night?'

'Did you stuff something up on your laptop again?' said the voice at the other end. 'I hear Kiri's your helpdesk now - she's very pleased she knows so much more than you do. Couldn't stop bragging about it when we went there for dinner a couple of weeks ago. You haven't got ransomware, have you?'

'Don't be an ass! Of course, not — I'd be screaming in panic if that was the case. But I'm helping a friend who's got on the wrong side of some neo-Nazis and Kiri wants to help, but I need you around to make sure she's safe.'

'Jesus, Ben! What are you getting yourself into? This sounds a bit dangerous — should you really involve Kiri?'

'Too late, already asked her, so how do we do this?'

After some discussion they agreed that Jonty would invite Kiri to his place and clear it with Ari before they started working.

'My place is better,' said Jonty, 'I have barriers around my systems that Kiri's never heard of. OK then, you give her the list and by the time she gets home, I'll have talked to Ari. I'll see if it's ok to work on it tonight, but don't bank on it, you know what Ari's like about homework and bedtimes.'

Mid-afternoon Ben got up from his chair where he had been sitting reading The Martian since lunchtime. 'We'll have to get you out of sight,' he said. 'I'm not risking that my favourite little snoop sees you here, not right now. She knows not to break a promise to me, but this might be too exciting not to hint at to her brothers or her mother, and I'd never hear the last of it. It's not something that's happened before. And if she sees you she might put two and two together and work out that you're the person who got me started on this, and I definitely don't want her to know that. I've already told her a story and a reason why I've got to keep this separate from work, partially true.'

He looked carefully at her, and she wondered what was coming next. Would he say she must temporarily go back to the container?

'So, could you please go into the third bedroom that I haven't even furnished, across the passage from your room. Take a book and stay there till she's gone? I usually keep the door closed, so to Kiri it will look the same as always. We'll put all your stuff in the wardrobe in your room.'

Emma spent half an hour moving everything from the table and making her room look unused, then shut herself in the empty third bedroom with a glass of water to wait for Kiri's arrival after school.

'No thanks, I don't need a chair,' she said, when Ben offered to move an armchair. 'I'll just take a couple of cushions and my Kindle, I'm halfway through a very interesting book.'

Kiri's arrival was noisy, and Emma listened to them greeting each other, the laughter and the excited questions about the project, as Kiri called it. She could hear the affection, imagined the hugs and was disappointed when their voices receded as they walked down the hallway. And then after a while, a loud shriek of excitement followed by an explosion of giggles, roused her from her reading.

'Oh, my God! Ben! There's girl stuff in the bathroom! Tell me!'

And then Ben's voice from the distance, 'So what? Can't I have a girl come over?'

And Kiri, still loud and excited, 'She must have been here overnight, there's shampoo and a hairbrush and all kinds of things on the windowsill. Is she gorgeous? Young or old?'

'She's totally gorgeous, very clever and yes, she did spend a night here.'

'Haha! Got you! One night? And she left all her stuff? Is she living here?'

'Let go of that doorhandle and come back here this instant!'

Emma smiled as she listened to Ben using his police officer voice and wondered if Kiri was going to obey.

'No snooping in my bedroom or there will be consequences – serious fallout. I mean it, Kiri! I insist on a bit of privacy. Now take this list and make sure you don't show anyone apart from Jonty. I have explained to him what kind of connections you'll be looking for. And don't do *any* social media searches until you're with him. If you handle this right he's promised he'll teach you things you've never heard of.

So, no risk-taking on your own before you're at Jonty's place, OK? And remember you can't share this story or anything from that list with your friends. I'll put the money directly into your bank account.'

Emma waited until she heard the front door close before she emerged. 'How much did you have to pay her?'

'She young enough to do anything for me for twenty dollars, mow the lawn, fix my phone and other stuff, but I'm giving her fifty this time. She's saving for a mountain bike, about half-way there. I might give it to her for Christmas – anything that stops her spending her entire life in front of a screen is good.'

Towards dinner time Emma decided to risk a rebuff and offered to make dinner, but Ben looked up from his book and said casually, 'Already ordered it so I hope you like pizza from that Italian place downtown. But you can cook tomorrow night if you like – I'll go and get anything you need in the morning. Or rummage around in the pantry and the fridge and see if we have enough to make something. Check the fridge first - I bought a truckload of raw materials and unloaded them before I went and picked you up.'

She was in the kitchen when Ben's phone buzzed and she heard him say, 'Hi there!' and then he came into the kitchen with the phone on speaker, put it on the table and said, 'Hang on – I don't think it's here. I certainly never used it, but I'll have a look in my top cupboards just in case.'

'Thanks, honey!' said a woman's voice, and Emma watched Ben climb on a kitchen chair and open a cupboard right up under the ceiling, then he called out, 'Not in the first one, I'll try the other one.'

'No, sorry! Not here.' He got off the chair and sat down on it by the table and left the phone on speaker, and the woman said, 'Oh, bugger! I must have stashed it in the garage when I moved. Now I'll have to get everything out, I really want to find it. The non-stick one isn't the same at all, things cook too quickly in the bottom of the pan.'

Ben laughed. 'What do you mean – garage? You live in an apartment, and you don't have a garage.'

'Don't be silly, darling,' said the woman. 'You know what I mean, the underground parking under the building. I always call it the garage. We all have a locker down there, about the size of a big wardrobe and I filled it up with random stuff when I moved in, and I haven't looked in it since.'

In Emma's head, questions she knew she would not be brave enough to ask, swirled while she continued to inspect what the pantry held. So, he did have a woman friend. Had she left some excess things in his house when she moved? She was obviously very fond of him, and he seemed very relaxed about letting Emma hear him talking to her. Be careful, she told herself, don't get too close to him, he was worried about you to start with, then he got concerned about those neo-Nazi guys, and now he's just a friend being kind. The fact that you're getting very attracted makes no difference, just keep your cool. That comment about staying here was probably just an offer to be a flatmate until my life's sorted out.

'Did you find anything?' Ben was still sitting at the kitchen table, but she hadn't realised he was watching her and hoped her face hadn't betrayed her thoughts or her change of mood.

'Plenty of useful things, I could easily make a nice dinner tomorrow. But truly, I should go home tomorrow morning, if you'll drive me over. There's no reason for me to stay here now.'

'Are you crazy? Of course, you're staying. I'm not letting you leave until this whole process is completed – when Jonty and Kiri find some material that we can use, he'll forward it anonymously with links and details to the right people. It might take a while before it spreads and becomes public knowledge so you're safe. I'm certain you're right about Miller, and we can't take any risks with that Brotherhood mob.'

'But you can't have me here all that time!' she protested trying to keep her voice unconcerned. 'It's ridiculous, I'll go to stay with mum and David in Tauranga.'

This was of course not going to happen, but she wasn't going to tell him that she couldn't afford to either drive or fly to Tauranga, because keeping money aside for a permanent move to the North Island was her escape hatch. She would pretend she was going to stay with her mother, but just quietly stay in the container and be very careful. He had done enough, and somehow she must leave without arousing any suspicions in his protective police officer mind.

'No way, you're not leaving,' he said firmly, but he was smiling. 'It's not negotiable. I want you here, so I know you're safe.'

OK, that didn't work, she thought, but this will, I'll remind him of his other commitments, and then he'll let me go.

'Your girlfriend won't like it,' she said casually. 'I mean, have you even told her I'm here, in the spare room? What if she pops in and get suspicious about who I'm really am? Unless you trust her with the real reason, of course.'

He looked at her with a smile lurking behind the serious mask and she could tell he was amused, really enjoying this.

'Have you been jumping to conclusions, Emma? That call was from my ex-wife who walked out on me about five years ago, no, very nearly six now. She's in a long-term, live-apart relationship with a *very* good-looking real estate agent, who's also trendy and drives a sportscar, *very* different from me. We're good friends now, far better than we were when we were married to each other. She thought I might have the cast-iron wok – but I don't, as you heard.'

Chapter 21

After breakfast the next morning Emma looked around her bedroom and mentally pictured how some of her own furniture could complete this nearly empty room, while at the same time telling herself not to get any ideas about a future that would probably never happen. But all the same, she could imagine her bedside table, the chest of drawers and maybe her small armchair making it a proper bedroom, instead of an empty room with a bed and a straight-backed kitchen chair. Since she woke up this morning, other similar thoughts had invaded her mind, like when she was wiping the kitchen table after breakfast and thought of the couple of hours she had spent in the totally empty third bedroom yesterday. A third room, unused and unfurnished and with no defined purpose. It could be a bedroom, of course or another guest room and she had the furniture to make that happen, or it could be a study.

While she made her bed, and tidied her clothes, a task that took two minutes, she told herself to avoid fantasies of that kind. They would serve no purpose other than to highlight what her life was like now, and how badly things had turned out. Being here was a period of respite, not the lead-in to a relationship. She put her sneakers on and went to find Ben, but he was nowhere to be seen until she went outside and met him coming towards the house with the large basket from beside the fireplace, now full of firewood.

'I'm coming in now. Could you hold the door for me? And don't stay out here, the wind's coming off the mountains, it's freezing. Or put your jacket on.'

She held the back door open and followed him inside, already shivering. 'How come this house stays warm all the time,' she asked as she watched him lay a fire in the fireplace, ready for the evening. 'These old houses are usually so hard to keep warm.'

'I bought the perfect house - spent nearly a year looking before I found what I wanted,' he said. 'And then this one came on the market. The previous owners had insulated it and double-glazed it and put solar panels on the roof, so I bought it. I hardly ever turn the panel heaters in the living room on because I like having a fire. It's exactly what I wanted. Do you want a cup of tea now?'

As she followed him to the kitchen, she smiled at

this morning's slightly different routine of coffee with breakfast and then a cup of tea, yesterday it was the other way around for no apparent reason. Instead of replying she said, 'Could I borrow your car this morning, please? If I'm staying another few days I need to pick up a couple of things from the container.'

'Let's have a cup of tea first and then I'll drive you over. We need to plan this. Is there another way to get to the container? Apart from that long track from the road, I mean.'

She took the mug he held out and sat down at the kitchen table, trying to imagine how she could get to the container from some other direction. She knew the reason for his question and agreed that it was a sensible precaution, but she had to admit defeat.

'I don't know − there might be a way, but I can't picture it.' And then it struck her. 'Of course, I can check it out on Google Earth.'

She pulled her laptop towards her from where it had sat since yesterday at the far end of the table, while Ben waited. Amazing, she thought as she typed in the address in the search bar. He never makes me feel rushed, I never feel he might be impatient while he waits like that, silent and still. It's so different from how I usually feel when someone's waiting for me to finish something, it often makes me nervous and then I fumble - but not with Ben.

'Come and have a look, so I don't have to describe it to you.' She pushed the laptop a bit to one side and

Ben came around and bent to look at it.

'See this road here, the one that leads to the rubbish transfer station, it skirts the fields behind the one the container's in. And there's the container, that rectangle, you can even see the little wooden platform outside the door if you zoom in.' She pointed at the edge of the large field behind Arnold's house. 'And that little square there, that's the out-house, it's been there for a long time. Might have been for the agricultural workers when Arnold leased out those fields to some vegetable grower long ago.'

'We could park over on the other side and walk across. We'll bring a bag and just quietly come and go without the old guy seeing you.'

To walk across the three large fields was not as easy as Emma had imagined and involved negotiating wire fences and to add to the difficulties, one of the fences was topped with a strand of barbed wire.

'Damn!' she said when she saw it. 'I can't get over that! My legs aren't long enough to straddle it safely. Maybe I'll have to go over to the side, but then I'll be on that other property with the horses, and the people who live there might get annoyed – or the horses might get annoyed.'

Ben dropped the bag over the fence, pushed the strand of barbed wire down with one hand and got a leg over, let go of the wire and held out a hand. 'Come here, stand just beside my leg and hold your arms out.'

God! The things I do just because he tells me to,

thought Emma, as she took up her position. This will be a disaster if he drops me, and I end up stuck on barbed wire like a soldier trying to cross into the enemy's trenches in the first world war.

'Arms,' said Ben, who had been watching her face, and she realised he was finding her expression funny. 'Hold them out.'

He bent sideways, took a firm hold of her waist with both hands, lifted her high and said, 'Now bend your knees so your feet clear the fence.' And seconds later she was over, and he followed.

'You're such a useful man,' she said and smiled up at him as they walked along the edge of the field. 'Like a human hoist. Who needs a stepladder when you're around? I really didn't expect that to work – I pictured myself hanging from the barbed wire screaming in agony.'

Ben grinned and said, 'Trust me, I know what I'm doing, said the superhero and started running, tripped on a turnip and twisted his ankle.'

The container felt icy cold and damp when Emma opened the sliding door. The contrast between this and Ben's house suddenly brought home how dramatically her life had changed from normal to nearly intolerable. It seemed incredible that everything in her life had crumbled in such a short time. While she collected another couple of books and some clothes, she thought again of her flat, that warm, light space and the lovely bathroom, and something inside her cracked. Since her daydreaming that morning, she had kept the image in her mind of her own flat the way it had been. Imagining her furniture in the nearly empty bedrooms at Ben's had somehow skewed the timeline, and her mind had reversed to when she still lived in the flat. She heard the sob before she realised she was about to cry, stopped herself by pure force of will and turned back to the bed as is she was looking at what she had assembled on the bed.

Ben appeared beside her and turned her towards him with one hand on her shoulder. 'What's wrong? What happened?'

'Nothing, don't worry,' she said and managed a smile. 'Just being silly – I remembered something.'

He dropped his hand and waited until the bag was packed, then she locked the sliding door again and they left the way they had come.

For the rest of the day Emma's mood was subdued. She worked on an assignment for a few hours after lunch, before she joined Ben in the living room as dusk descended, and it was time to light the fire and draw the curtains.

The book he was reading lay open on the table by his chair, and she picked it up, still The Martian. 'Are you enjoying this?'

'Totally! Far superior to the film. I think it's all the detail about how he works things out, from a science point of view. In the film you don't get that in the same way, or only sketchily.'

'I read the book first and then I watched the movie, and I thought the same thing. I think it's the science that involves me so strongly in the book, the explanations about how he solves the problems and all the interesting perspectives you get. His mental calculations, how he's affected by his situation, how he manages the practical aspects of all those improvisations he's forced to make. The film didn't give the same depth.'

Abruptly Ben changed the mood, looking at her in a way she suspected meant that he was intent on finding something out. 'What happened in the container this morning?'

'Oh, just a memory,' she said vaguely, trying to sound casual. 'I'm over it now, nothing to worry about.'

She hoped her face didn't reflect what she felt, because now that she knew him so much better and understood him, to some degree at least, she was sure he was concerned enough to pursue it. Instead of replying, he got up from his chair and came around to the sofa.

'Would you stand up, please?' he said, and when she hesitated he repeated it. 'Please?'

She got slowly to her feet, and he said, 'Come here,' and pulled her to him, once again holding her against his chest with his hands on her back. And once again she leaned her face into his shoulder, and after a moment she relaxed against him and sighed.

'Thank you.' She said it very quietly, as if she was

talking to herself, and he held her for a moment longer before he let his hands drop and went back to his chair.

The looked at each other across the coffee table and exchanged a little smile; comforting on his side and grateful on hers. How extraordinary, thought Emma, that he can feel the need to comfort me without asking any more questions or saying anything, what a wonderful talent – he just made me feel so much better.

Late on Friday afternoon, after spending some time texting or emailing on his phone, Ben said, 'Jonty and Kiri are coming over straight after dinner. He says they have news, and they're expecting ice cream and wine.'

'Or wine for him and ice cream for Kiri? Am I allowed to be present this time?'

'Of course. I've just told him not to tell Kiri that you'll be here. I want to give her a surprise and strong warning about keeping this secret when she gets here, and I've got a favour to ask of you.'

'I can't imagine how I could do *you* a favour.' Emma laughed. 'All the favours have been going in the other direction so far, and I've got nothing to give. But take it as read that I'll do whatever it is.'

'You might not want to, but I hope you'll do it. I think the most effective way to make Kiri remember to keep absolutely everything about this whole saga to herself, is for you to tell her about what happened at the river - and what it did to you.'

'Everything?' Could she do this a second time? Could she cope with reliving the terror, fearing for her life and the lonely freezing trek through the forest, not even sure she was going in the right direction. It sent a chill down her spine to even contemplate re-telling the details.

Ben had been watching her face while she thought. 'Yes, all of it, every horrific detail. I know it took a toll on you when you told me, but I think it's the key. Hearing how brutal and terrifying it was, and how you knew there was only one way out, to throw yourself into that freezing water and how you thought you were drowning.'

Emma thought for only a moment longer before she admitted to herself that he was right. For a fourteen-year-old to hear it directly from her would be very powerful, a perfect demonstration of how dangerous the Brotherhood guys were, and she knew Ben would be there to intervene if the situation looked like getting out of control.

'OK, I'll do it. I see your point, it would be effective – but you've got to be there, don't leave me alone with her.'

'Of course.' He said nothing more about it. They had an early meal that Emma prepared and had just finished putting things in the dishwasher when the doorbell went.

'Come in and meet Emma,' she heard Ben say when he went to open the door. 'Kiri, would you please take those boots off before you go any further?'

Emma, who had imagined Kiri to be small and bubbly, after the burbling cheerfulness she had heard of Kiri's and Ben's exchanges a few days ago, was surprised to find herself saying hi to a skinny teenager who was taller than she was. Kiri, with dark brown eyes just like her uncle Ben's, with dark hair and a scarlet fringe, studied her carefully, said 'hi' then turned to her uncle with a sly smile. 'Oh, well done, Ben!'

Emma smothered laughter at the look on Ben's face, but there was no time to comment, because Jonty was already unloading things on the kitchen table and saying something to Ben, who still had a slightly stunned expression on his face. Perhaps just as well Jonty didn't hear that, thought Emma, or Ben might have had to explain a whole raft of things that Kiri simply took as given.

'Let's have a glass of wine,' she said now and moved towards the fridge. Ben followed with Kiri and asked if she wanted wine or ice cream. 'Are you for real?' said Kiri. 'Can I?'

'No, just teasing,' said Ben and laughed. 'About time I got a hit in, don't you think?'

'Now or after?' Emma said quietly to Ben, while he opened the wine bottle and Jonty was saying something to Kiri.

'Later,' he said out of the corner of his mouth. 'Sit opposite her, beside me.'

'Now, then,' said Ben when they had seated themselves at the table, Kiri and Jonty beside each other across from Emma and himself. 'How do you want to do this, Jonty? Do you want the full story from Emma, about how this started, or would you rather tell us what you've found?'

Jonty glanced at Kiri. 'I think miss smarty-pants here should tell you what we found so far. And I'll say this only once, Kiri, in case your head gets so big you can't get out the door. You have amazed me, little niece. I had no idea how clever and well informed you are. From now on we'll do some stuff together now and then.' He drank some of his wine and looked at Ben. 'And you and I will have to keep an eye on her. You realise that, don't you? She's got the brains to become a cyber terrorist and we'll get the blame.'

'Haha, very funny!' said Kiri and pushed her elbow hard into her uncle's ribs. 'But yeah, I'd like to tell them, thanks — this whole thing was radical, uber exciting. And we've found links between that Miller guy in Auckland and not just the Brotherhood but several other groups as well, a couple of kind of mad groups where people just want to — what's that thing about government, Jonty?'

'They want to make the country ungovernable,' said Jonty. 'Fucking morons!'

'Yeah, that was it, ungovernable, sounds crazy. It would be chaos, wouldn't it? Anyway, we've put it all together with lots of links into a kind of report, and we've sent it to four genuine antifa groups, two here, one in Australia and one in Canada - and they'll get it out further.'

'We've got their word that they'll send the report to all major news media, post it in social media and get it shared,' said Jonty. 'They won't mention where it came from – and let's face it, they don't know. I set up an untraceable email address, well not completely untraceable, but it could only be traced back to me by an expert, and the antifa groups won't do that, they're on our side. They can follow the links I've given them and check the information we've given them is correct, and then they'll get it out to a wider audience, as Kiri said. It will be impossible for media or bloggers to work out where this originated once it starts spreading. And I'm in anonymous touch with a couple of influential bloggers too. I think you're perfectly safe from anyone thinking it came from you. Once it proliferates it will be impossible to work out where it started.'

Ben and Emma looked at each other and she said, 'Wow! We would never have got that right. We would have left ourselves wide open to retaliation. I'm so grateful to you both!'

Ben raised his glass. 'Thanks! Great work from the new team! And now I suppose there are only a couple of things left – waiting for the media to take it up, and Miller's reaction, that's the first thing and I'm really looking forward to that.'

'Ah, yes, another thing,' said Jonty. 'The report I've

compiled, I printed it out for you.' He looked seriously at Ben. 'I printed it, because none of this is going to be sent as email between us, of course. I'll leave a copy for you, and make sure you check the amazing list of the nine fake identities Miller uses to fuel anger and stir up trouble in social media. He posts things under fake identities and praises Gerald Miller as the voice of reason in a troubled world– on every social media site you can imagine and in those private groups. He's a one-man troublemaking unit, that guy. Must spend hours posting all that stuff and keeping track of what he's said in which media. Incredible – but Kiri tells me she's impressed with how inventive he is with his online names.'

'Can we please see the letter?' asked Kiri, turning to Emma. 'I'd love to see it. Ben said all this started with an old letter – how you found out, I mean.'

'I want Emma to tell you how this came about,' said Ben, 'including perhaps showing you the letter. Did you bring it?'

'I'll get it out in a moment,' said Emma, who had put the letter on the kitchen windowsill just before their visitors arrived. 'But here's how it started.'

It took three quarters of an hour before it was done: telling the story, answering endless questions, trying to satisfy requests for more details and passing the letter and envelope from hand to hand. She left out any mention of having to give up her flat or living in the container; those things were deeply personal and talking about it in front of two virtual strangers was a step too far.

'Awesome story!' said Kiri and got up to help herself to more ice cream. 'You must have spent hours doing all the research. I'd never heard of that Paperspast website, I must go and have a look.'

Emma glanced sideways at Ben, hoping that maybe he would have changed his mind about what he wanted her to tell Kiri, but he waited for Kiri to sit down again and said, 'And now for the serious stuff.'

He leaned forward over the table and spoke directly to Kiri. 'What Emma's going to tell you is traumatic for her to talk about, and she's only going to do it because I want us all to be reminded of how dangerous this would be if one of us becomes linked to it. And it means that when it breaks in the media, you can't ever, not by one single word or a wink, imply you know anything more than other people! Do you understand?'

There's the police officer voice again, thought Emma and watched Kiri looking mesmerised across the table at Ben, her eyes wide.

'God, no! Of course, I won't! Now that I've seen how scary those online groups are, I'd rather die than let on I was involved in outing them. Ben, I promise!'

They all looked at Emma now, and she tried to think where to start, but the simplest thing was to begin with her decision about wanting to be outside in the sunshine, however cold. She avoided mentioning the shipping container and just said she had wanted an outing somewhere in the country instead of going for a walk in town.

When she got to the point where the SUV drove into the parking area at the river she hesitated and glanced briefly at Ben before she continued.

'Two guys got out and they came straight towards me, as if they were on a mission, and I began to feel a bit worried. The place is only partially visible from the road and there was nobody else there, but I had no time to take any kind of evasive action. They were between me and my car, so I stayed where I was – on that flat rock at the edge of the pool.'

She looked at Ben again and he nodded. Kiri's eyes had followed their exchange and she was beginning to look apprehensive, as if she sensed a threat hanging in the air between them.

'They kind of hemmed me in, one on each side of me, and one of them grabbed hold of my arm. They said they knew I had found a book and a letter, and I had to give it to them, and also my phone - and I must promise never to talk about it again.' She swallowed. 'Or they would first break my arms, one at a time, then my legs and throw me in the river and watch me drown.'

She felt Ben's warm hand on her thigh under the table, pulled herself together and continued.

'And I knew they could do what they said. They

were cold, kind of hard and focused without a trace of empathy, merciless. They said the Brotherhood would see to it I didn't disobey, and I believed them.'

She paused again, took a sip of her wine and felt Ben's hand grip her thigh tighter. 'So, I threw myself in the water and swam across that deep pond to the river itself. It was a struggle, my clothes got very heavy and kind of dragged me down, it was slow and hard. The water was freezing, and when I first went in it felt like I'd been thumped really hard in the chest, as if my heart would stop beating. And then the current caught me, and I realised I might drown.' She looked again at Ben, and he nodded.

'The river was very high, and the current was fast, where it hit rocks it foamed and sprayed. It took hold of me and tumbled me over and over. It forced me way down - I needed to breathe but I couldn't get up to the surface, I was being rolled along the bottom. I thought I was going to die, no, I *knew* I was going to die - but then suddenly my head was in the air again, and I'd been swept way down the river. After a while I was so exhausted I was on the verge of giving up, because my clothes made it so hard to swim and I didn't think I could stay afloat much longer, and I was ready to give up. But somehow I managed to get closer to the other side, where they couldn't get to me. I got smashed up against a rock close to the bank and I lay there for a while, half in and half out of the water and got my breath back. And then I struggled out and started walking through the bush – to get out of sight in case they walked along the other side looking for me.'

'Jesus!' said Jonty. 'What an ordeal - you poor thing! How on earth did you get home? I'm surprised you didn't die. That river must have been freezing cold – it starts way up in the mountains.'

'How did they know to follow you there?' asked Kiri. 'Maybe there's a tracker on your car? If they found out you work at the library and then where you live, they could have put one on.'

'I'm sure you're right,' said Ben. 'It's the only realistic explanation I've been able to think of. And amazingly Emma remembers the rego on that SUV, so I'll make it my business to find out who owns it. I can't do anything about what they did to Emma without exposing her, but I'd like to know whose car it is. But let me tell you what happened next.'

His hand gave her thigh a little pat and appeared on the edge of table again. 'I'd been out to visit great-auntie Annie, remember her, Kiri? Or you might not have met her since you were a toddler, actually. I don't think she's left her house for ten years, Jordan does her shopping. Never mind, she lives thirty or so kilometres up that road on the far side of the river, you turn off the main road at the curved bridge just before you start the climb up the hill. So, there I was at dusk, driving back to town and I saw a woman walking along the side of the road, and when I got closer I realised her clothes and hair were wet and she was just trudging along as if she was exhausted. And I couldn't figure out where she'd come from and how she got wet. The road where I saw her is a long way from the river and there are no houses anywhere near.'

He reached for the wine bottle and topped up their glasses and nobody said a word, their eyes fixed on him. 'It was very cold that day and the wind was getting stronger, not to mention that it would be dark pretty soon. I slowed down beside her, wound the window down and offered her a lift, and she said, "No thanks," with hardly a glance at me and continued walking. So, I drove along beside her and said she looked very cold, and it was dangerous for her to be on the road in the dark, anything could happen to her. And she said, very sarcastic and with her teeth chattering with cold, "Yeah, like someone might drive alongside me in a car and try to get me into it?" And continued walking.'

Kiri stared; her eyes rimmed with dark eyeliner wide open, full of awe. 'You told him to fuck off? And leave you freezing to death on that road in the dark?'

'Basically, yes − I didn't know he wasn't some Brotherhood guy they'd sent out to find me on that side of the river, so I turned him down. I'd had enough of strangers.'

Ben chuckled. 'And then this amazing girl finally accepted a ride − after I got out and walked beside her to show her my police ID. And what did she do? First she asked if I had locked my car before walking off down the road after her, then she finally looked at my badge *and* took a photo of it with her phone, which turned out to be waterproof. She was shaking uncontrollably, her lips were blue, and she could hardly get the words out. I was seriously worried about her. That's why she's here now.'

Jonty frowned. 'Here, as in staying here for some time, I hope? I think she should be kept out of the public eye until this story breaks in the media.'

'Of course,' said Ben, clearly not about to tell them anything about the container or how he put her to bed there and sat for hours watching over her.

'She's in my badly equipped spare room and she's not going anywhere – at least not without me beside her until this whole thing's safely out in the public arena and there's no point in the Brotherhood trying to silence and punish her.'

When Jonty and Kiri finally left it was nearly eleven o'clock and Emma felt exhausted. When they said goodbye on the front step Kiri hugged Emma tight without saying anything and Emma held her for a moment and said quietly, 'Thank you!'

They spent a long time over breakfast on Saturday morning, reading and discussing the report that Jonty had left a printed copy of, after a final warning to not under any circumstances look up any of the social media accounts mentioned in it.

'Just don't, please!' he had said when he handed it over, just as he and Kiri were leaving, his voice deadly serious. 'Some of those links are to private groups and you don't want your online identities anywhere near them. Kiri and I did the work on one of my laptops, but under layers of protection that neither of you have. Just read the report and wait for stage two to explode in the media.'

Now, Ben looked across the table at Emma and said, 'I didn't realise Jonty could prove that Miller is the same person as all those identities he assumed when he pretends to be someone else – I bet Miller never thought his ISP address was such a dangerous thing.'

'Neither did I. What incredible luck that your sister happens to have a brother-in-law who's such an expert - we could never have done it on our own. And what's this antifa thing? They mentioned it when they were here and I've seen it here and there, but I never looked it up.'

'It's the abbreviated term for groups that fight against the fascist and neo-Nazi groups, organise counter demonstrations and that sort of thing. It's short for anti-fascist.'

Emma thought for a moment, trying to remember where she had seen it last and then she realised that one of the men on the riverbank had used it. 'Those guys at the river used it, they said they knew I was antifa. And you know what? I've just remembered the exact phrase they used about the Brotherhood, too. They said I had to do what they said, "because the Brotherhood defends its own" – so that's a pretty close an admission that my Miller search had touched a nerve with them.'

'How do you feel about it now? After telling the story again yesterday, I mean.'

Why is he asking? wondered Emma, is he worried I'll have a retroactive meltdown? He's very protective, which I'm not used to and never thought I'd like, but it's nice feeling that someone's got my back.

'I'm OK now,' she said. 'And thanks for being supportive yesterday in a hands-on kind of way, if you'll excuse the pun. What would you have done if I'd started panicking like I did the first time I told you?'

'Oh, just the same old thing,' he said, and there was that hidden amusement again. 'I would have grabbed you and held you tight and made sure you knew you were safe. Nothing spectacular.'

'Really? In front of Jonty and Kiri?' She was sure he was teasing, but he surprised her.

'Of course, I would. Your state of mind is more important than what they might think.'

Despite the initially bantering style of their exchange, she suddenly felt she must make sure he knew how deeply grateful she was, and how important he had been over the last week.

'Listen Ben,' she said, her voice serious now. 'I want

you to know that your support – in every way and every time I've needed it, is something I'll treasure.' She hesitated for a short moment and continued before she had time to change her mind. 'It's been a while since I've felt I wasn't utterly alone, at the bottom of a pit. I know how I lived was a self-imposed isolation, it could have been avoided, and now I can see in retrospect that I was in a kind of bubble of independence, a voluntary loneliness. You've made me feel so different.'

He looked at her for so long she started to feel embarrassed and thought that maybe she had overstepped the mark, that he might think she was being too emotional, then he said, 'That was my intention. Emma, right from the start out there on that dark road.'

He got up with his plate in his hand and walked around behind her to take hers, bent down and kissed the top of her head and once again left her unable to look at him. When she did look up he was putting things in the dishwasher and filling the electric jug again, and she smiled just as he turned his head in her direction. Ben smiled back and nothing more was said about it.

Chapter 22

A couple of days later Ben returned from the front door just after seven with three newly delivered boxes of take-away Thai food, Emma said, '*Three* lots of Thai food - is someone joining us for dinner?'

'Don't be silly – I eat at least twice as much as you and I had no idea what you like, forgot to ask, so ordering three different meals seemed sensible. Plenty of choice.'

They ate in the living room with the fire blazing and Emma thought that she would treasure the memory of this interlude when she was back in the container: the leaping flames behind the glass in the fireplace, being in a warm, comfortable room and the feeling of complete safety. Those things were not hers by right, they were borrowed comfort, but for the moment she could revel in it.

'Are you happy?' asked Ben when they had disposed

of the mess from dinner, but she had no idea what the question referred to and replied semi-evasively, 'At this very moment I couldn't be happier.'

The look he slanted sideways at her was hard to read, but she thought he probably got it; she was not going to say she was generally or usually happy, just that tonight she was definitely happy. And then his next question took her by surprise and made her wonder why it hadn't occurred to her that he was bound to ask this at some stage.

'That little chair you brought with you? Was it yours when you were a little girl?'

Did he really think that, or was he just giving her the chance to say it was, and get out of explaining anything else? She had to tell him because this wasn't a thing she would lie about.

'It was Lily's - my daughter who died when she was two. Three years ago, next month.'

The room was so silent now it felt as if time had stopped and after a pause he said, 'What happened? An accident?'

'You could call it that, I suppose,' she said with a wry smile. 'It was classed as an accidental death. My partner, Lily's father, ran her over on the driveway outside our house. He was cleaning the car and had her with him, he was supposed to look after her on Saturday mornings while I worked. It was a safe garden, and the gate was shut, so all he had to do was keep an eye on what she was doing. But he got in the car to move it a few meters and he was talking to someone on the phone at the same time - he reversed over her and crushed her chest. She died instantly.'

Ben got up from his armchair without saying a word and sat down on the sofa beside her. He put his arm around her shoulders, and she leaned into him, grateful for the lack of voiced commiseration or comment, comfortable to just sit and to be held. They stayed like that for a long time, close together, not moving, just looking at the flames dancing in the fireplace, then Emma said, 'I don't know why that chair is so important to me. My mum gave it to Lily for her second birthday, not long before she died, and she loved it, she used to drag it around so she could sit in it wherever we were. She'd sit there very straight and rest her arms on the arms of the chair — she looked so cute.'

Ben pulled her closer and kissed her temple. 'Have you got a photo you can show me?'

Emma picked up her phone from the table and opened the album called "Lily" and handed it to him. 'If you scroll through to the fourth or fifth image you'll see her sitting in that chair watching a cartoon on TV. It was the perfect size for someone her age, and my mum let her pick the fabric for the cushion she made.' Emma smiled at the memory. 'Mum was sure Lily would pick something with cartoon figures or perhaps hens — she loved hens, but she picked a very traditional flowery one.'

'And then your relationship split? As they often do after tragedies where someone feels guilty.'

'He moved out two weeks after the funeral.' She paused and her hands clenched on her lap. 'The night before he left, he said I should be grateful I was at work that morning and didn't see it. He said, "I'll have to live with the memory forever, it's my punishment". And now I hear he's practically an alcoholic. I didn't have the mental strength at the time to try to work through it with him, to help him as well as myself. I just let him go. I was too traumatised. He still lives in Taupo where we were living at the time, so now and then someone mentions him.'

'Did you forgive him?'

She had to think about it. Did she ever say that she forgave him, did he ever ask her to forgive him? No, she didn't think that word formed part of any conversation she had with him after the accident, few though these were, and short.

'At the time the word forgive was never mentioned, but I don't think I ever said it was his fault or blamed him, and I never asked him why he hadn't kept an eye on where she was either. I only started thinking about that much later – that his negligence was what he was having to live with, as well as that dreadful sight. He did say that, but at the time it didn't really register.'

She thought for a moment, trying to recall details of that blurred time, the few weeks after the day she was taken aside at work and found a female police officer waiting to talk to her. She thought of how she went back to the house and the drive was wet where it had happened, where someone had hosed the blood off before she could see it. The way she had walked around the wet patch as if she couldn't bear to step on it and continued to do so until she moved away.

'I don't think I spoke more than ten words on any one day from that Saturday until about a month later. I was numb, most of it is a blur now. I took leave and just sat in the park down by the lake looking towards the volcanoes with my brain idling. Now, when I look back, it seems incredible that I never blamed him to his face at the time.'

'Do you still love him?'

'No, I don't. I realised a while after the accident, when I had kind of recovered my ability to think, that if I *had* loved him enough I would have made an effort to stop him leaving – as it was, I let him go, as he clearly wanted to. I have no idea if he really loved me, but I was obviously going to be a constant reminder for him, make him feel guilty even if I never said anything. I think there probably wasn't enough genuine love there before the accident, so afterwards it just died completely.'

'You're an incredible girl,' said Ben and tightened his arm around her shoulders. 'As I said to Jonty and Kiri - I knew it straight away when we talked through the car window on the road, and you managed to come up with cutting remarks, even though your lips were blue, and you were shivering with cold. And then when you checked if I had locked the car before walking away from it, telling your rescuer off – epic! To be able to use sarcasm in such a crushing way, when you were nearly hypothermic and had no idea how far you had to walk. It was unbelievable.'

Now she laughed. 'If there was anything incredible about me that day, it was how incredibly rude and hostile I was to someone who was trying to help me. And I continued to be rude and hostile when you followed me home, too. There was no end to my ingratitude, was there?'

'You don't get it, do you?' he said and gave her a little shake before he got up. 'I never thought of you as rude and hostile, I thought you were amazing, and I decided there and then that I wanted to look after you, preferably forever, you stroppy, independent girl.'

He rose and went to the kitchen, leaving her sitting there not knowing quite what to think. It was difficult to imagine he was serious, but this wasn't the first time he had said it. He was so unlike any man she'd ever known, she thought, and looked absently at the pattern the flames threw on the polished wood floor in front of the fireplace. He was complex and easy to understand at the same time. Very direct at times and then prepared to wait patiently without comment at other times. Very physical but also gentle. She remembered the feel of his hands on her frozen feet and the way he had made sure she was properly tucked in. Was he really serious? She felt she could love this man forever. She hadn't fallen in love with him, she just loved him, though she couldn't explain the difference. Did she dare respond the way she wanted to? Or should she brush it off and just wait, stay safe from some future disappointment, from being let down?

'Here you are,' said Ben when he returned with two glasses of wine. 'I think we need some more of this. So, are you?'

'Am I what?'

'Going to stay with me forever, of course.'

'Ben, are you totally crazy or is this your mad sense of humour again? We've only known each for a few days.'

'For God's sake, girl! Would I joke about something like this? Of course, I mean it – time has nothing to do with it. But you don't have to answer right now, tomorrow morning will do if you need more time to think about it.'

Again, she sensed that secret amusement, though how she knew was hard to say. His expression didn't change, his voice was calm and neutral still, he just stood there beside the coffee table and waited. She got a strange feeling that he knew her answer before she did, that he had sensed something in her during these last few days that had told him … something.

And then, surprising them both, she raised her glass and said cheerfully, 'Of course I'll stay with you forever. I can't think of anything nicer.'

He took the glass out of her hand and put it on the table alongside his own. 'Come here,' he said and pulled her against him. His hands found their way under her sweatshirt and the feel of them, warm against the skin on her back, slowly moving from her ribcage down to her waist and holding her tight against him, made her tempted to say, 'Let's go to bed now!' but she didn't. She hadn't felt like this since Lily died, and she wanted to treasure the moment, just stand there and feel his body reacting to her and know that pleasure and joy were possible, after all.

When he finally let go of her, he handed her the glass he had taken out of her hand, and said, 'See what I mean? That's what I mean by incredible – you took me totally by surprise then, left me speechless. And here I was thinking I'd have to work on you for weeks to make you see that you'll never find anyone who'll love you more than I do. I knew it right away – very strange, really, not the kind of thing I've ever believed in, and certainly not anything I thought would happen to me. I mean, I'm not that kind of guy, not romantic.'

Emma woke in the middle of the night, with her back against Ben's chest and his arm over her middle and sensed that he was awake too.

'Are you awake?' she whispered, just in case he wasn't, and he pulled her closer against him and said, 'Are you uncomfortable? Is my arm too heavy?'

'Oh no, please leave it just where it is – it's nice,' said Emma and smiled into the dark. 'I just suddenly woke up for some reason.'

'So, no regrets?' His voice was as usual neutral and giving no clue to why he was asking. 'You still have a choice, of course. We got quite emotional last night, and you might need more time.'

'To do what?'

'To think about this, decide if it's really what you want. I'll still help you get out of that bloody container and whatever you need, but you might want to regard this a temporary – us, I mean.'

She turned under his arm and knew that now it was important to do this right, unmoved by sudden emotion and lust. 'Do *you* want it to be temporary?'

She felt certain he didn't. The way he had told her how he felt the previous evening had left no doubt in her mind, but she felt obliged to ask the question, then she continued without waiting for an answer.

'I think this is it for me – the thing I never really believed would happen,' she said and put her hand on his face, rubbed her thumb over the stubble, and smiled again. 'I never really thought that stuff about true love was true. Not that I didn't fall in love, of course I did, but the concept of deep abiding love that could outlast anything – I thought it was probably just wishful thinking when people wrote or talked about it. And ...' She paused, tried to think about the most factual way to say it.

'And?' said Ben, and she knew this was a crucial moment in their relationship. 'And now I do,' she said, her fingers moving lightly over his cheek. 'I really and truly do – love you, I mean. I thought about it last night, how strange this is – I didn't fall in love, there was no transition at all, no gradual realisation, I just suddenly knew I'll love you forever, as ridiculous as that might sound.'

He pulled her even closer and kissed her forehead. 'Me too, perfect. Seeing we're wide awake now, would you like a cup of tea? Or some ice cream?'

She laughed. 'You're unique, do you know that? I've thought it several times – I've never met anyone like you, and honestly, I don't think there is anyone else like you. I've got the only one – perfect! But ice cream in the middle of the night?'

'I know,' he said, and she both heard and felt his quiet chuckle. 'Terrible habit – we'll have to watch it, or we'll become addicted and *fat*. I don't normally eat ice cream if I wake up in the middle of the night, I just have a cup of tea and read for a while. But maybe we could regard it as a celebration – and then we could ...'

'What could we? Oh, wait! I know something we could do after the ice cream, or before ...'

In the morning she turned from the toaster when Ben appeared fully dressed after his shower and she said, as if not believing what she saw. 'You got dressed? Aren't we going back to bed?' And then she added quickly, when he looked as if he was about to start pulling his t-shirt over his head. 'Stop it, you know I'm kidding! Let's have breakfast and I'll have a shower straight after. And I do need a shower too after all that sweaty activity in the night.'

'So, what's next?' asked Ben and watched her spread peanut butter on a slice of toast. 'Is that for me?'

'No,' said Emma firmly, 'it's for me. I'll do one for you if you want me to, but this is what I have every morning – one slice of wholemeal toast with peanut butter. It sets me up for the day. And what *is* next? Lots of things, but what comes first?'

'I was thinking about it in the shower. Not that it's for me to decide, but I thought we'd start sorting out your stuff. I sent an email to work yesterday and said I'd like to take a week's leave – very short notice, but they know I never normally do this kind of thing, and I often cover for others. You know, when they have sick partners or kids or other emergencies. So, they said yes.'

'It's for us to decide together what's next, I think. Its not for me to decide what to add to this house.' Emma took another bite of her toast, put the half-eaten piece on her plate, and reached for the butter, well aware that Ben was watching her hand and probably thinking she was going to prepare another piece of toast for herself to have straight after first.

'Tell me what you think we should do first.' She put the lid back on the peanut butter jar and handed him the slice of toast, and he laughed.

'Don't do that too often, I might get used to it. But my idea was that we get a big trailer and go to that storage shed so you can decide what you want to bring here. We've got one totally empty bedroom, one that's barely furnished, and we can decide if your table is better than mine and so on. Maybe you want to have the empty bedroom as a study? Maybe you like your sofa better than mine?'

'Heavens, Ben! Don't let's change a single thing in the living room, I love it. The colours are great, and I already think of that sofa corner as my personal property. Who decorated the place?'

'Kiri and I went together and raided a furniture place when I bought this house. She was ten or eleven and I'd been living in a smallish flat for a couple of years after my wife left. Kiri condemned my stuff from the flat as total rubbish.' He smiled at the memory. 'For a kid that age to take charge and tell me that the most important thing for me was to start with new things and not drag my old life into this house – I was stunned at her perception. She's an amazing little girl – well, a big girl now.'

'I've got an idea,' said Emma. 'Very devious, and it involves lying or at least implying something that isn't true. You know how I said that I've told nobody I'm living in a container – you're the only one who knows.'

She couldn't quite meet his eyes, unsure of how he would react when she told him the reason. 'Somehow I couldn't bear to admit what things had come to, so I pretended to everyone I'd got a tiny studio flat on the outskirt of town, explained about the rent increase, said I couldn't afford to keep my nice place. It was a kind of self-protective thing. And the only people outside of this city who know I lost my job are my mum and my friend Catriona, who's a lawyer, I asked her for some advice.' She smiled. 'You'll realise when you meet my mum that she's very hard to fool, so I had to tell her before she started on a third degree-type interrogation. I used the redundancy as a reason, pretended it was true, so she wouldn't be so upset.'

'You really isolated yourself, didn't you? I thought that might be it when I realised how you were living. I spent a lot of time thinking while I sat there watching you sleep. I wish I'd known you earlier, I would have helped you.' He smiled across the table, and she knew he understood why she had done it, and the relief was immediate because she had been worried about how crazy it would sound.

'I've got to know who's been told what,' said Ben. 'I need to get it clear in my head. Your mum thinks you moved to that fictitious studio flat, and so does your friend Anne, but what about Fletcher? You said he couldn't help with a job – did you confess about the container to him? You seem very close.'

'No, I didn't tell him. He would have got upset

about it and felt he should do something, but it wasn't his problem. We *are* close, and though he wished he could, he couldn't invent a job for me at the lodge – not when everyone knew there was no vacancy. There was nothing he could do, so telling him was just going to upset him on my behalf. And our closeness is not from some past relationship, just in case you're wondering. He's gay and wouldn't kiss a girl unless you paid him.'

'Oh, good,' said Ben ambiguously. 'So, the second thing or maybe the first, is to empty the container while we have the trailer. One load to come here and one to go somewhere else like the Salvation Army store or the Women's Refuge or something like it. How does that sound?'

'We won't need a trailer for what I want out of the container, your car will do – let's start with the container and go as soon as I've had my shower.'

Chapter 23

As soon as they turned into the lane beside Arnold's house Ben stopped and they stared in dismay, because what they saw was the fire blackened shell of the container with crime scene tape around it. The ranch-slider door seemed to have blown out, and even from a distance it was obvious that the interior must be totally destroyed.

Emma jumped out of the car and ran forward crunching over blackened glass shards to peer in. There was nothing there apart from small heaps of sooty remains, one glance was enough to tell her that there was nothing left to be salvaged.

Ben came up behind her and put his arm over her shoulders, held her close. 'Those bastards! Thank God you weren't here.'

He let her go and walked around the side of the container and came back looking grim. 'They torched the car as well,' he said and got his phone out.

Emma put a hand on his arm, alarmed. 'What are you doing? Are you calling the police?'

He put the phone back in his pocket. 'Listen! This has gone far enough. There's no danger to you in reporting that this might be linked to those guys at the river. We don't have to mention that damn Brotherhood group or anything related to it. They can't be allowed to get away with arson, they've crossed the line now. We'll come up with a way of explaining it. Let's go and ask the old man what he knows and then I'll call in and check what they know downtown.'

Emma thought through the implications of reporting that she might know who had don't this, tried to come to terms with it becoming police business, and reluctantly admitted he was right.

'OK, you're right. If they think they'll get away with this, they'll think they can do whatever they like in the future. Let's go and talk to Arnold.'

She noticed Ben's sideways glance at her and said, 'Don't worry, Ben! There's no meltdown coming up. I left nothing special or valuable here when you took me to your place. My favourite books are lost, but they can be replaced − or not.' She gave him a little smile. 'And you know it's true, you saw it for yourself. It was minimally furnished, so it's not a tragedy. I was just shocked they had done this. I think you've saved my life twice now. I'll have to buy some clothes, but what of it?'

'Good girl!' said Ben as they turned to walk done the track again and took her hand.

'There you are!' exclaimed Arnold when he opened the door. 'I've been so worried. I had to tell the police I didn't know how to contact you. All I knew was that you'd be away for a few days. This is your friend who took you to the bus, is it? Come in!'

'So, the police obviously know about this,' said Ben when they were seated on an ancient sofa covered in patterned velvet with crochet rugs folded over both arms. 'We saw the crime scene tape. When did it happen?'

'Oh, yes,' said the old man. 'I called the fire brigade when I noticed the flames and the police came soon after. I felt so stupid when I couldn't even tell them your full name, Emma. I never thought to ask what your surname was when you first came.'

'I'm so sorry this happened while I was away and caused you so much worry!' Emma felt she should apologise, though he seemed to have stood up to the excitement very well, nearly enjoyed the drama. 'Luckily I had nothing valuable in there, just the bare minimum, so nothing precious is lost. Oh, sorry, I must introduce you, this is Ben, Arnold.'

They didn't stay long, but when they left Ben told Arnold he would organise for the car to be removed. 'I can get the container moved too,' he said. 'Once the forensics people have finished with it.'

'No, no, don't you bother with that,' said Arnold comfortably. 'Get the car taken away, it's like having rubbish there, but don't fuss about the container. It can sit there and rust and become a kind of monument. I'll get my son-in-law to get rid of the glass, he's got a trailer so he can take it to the dump. I might ask him to knock down the outhouse too.'

Ben reversed out of the track, parked further down the road and got his phone out again while Emma tried to think of plausible ways of relating what had happened at the river without making it sound crazy.

'Hi, Sandra,' said Ben. 'Can you tell me what we know about that container that caught fire – the one in a field behind a house in Sandy Road. Is it your case?'

He listened for a long time before he said anything else. Emma could hear the voice at the other end talking fast but not what she said, and she was getting more curious by the minute, but as usual Ben's face revealed nothing.

'OK, listen,' Ben said finally. 'The person who lived there is a friend of mine, Emma Stewart, she was away for a few days, thank God. We're coming in for her to make a statement, and she's got some useful information for you.'

He finished the call and started the car. 'Let's take this one step at a time,' he said calmly, but by now she could tell that secret amusement behind the casual tone. 'We'll not call you my partner, we'll stick with you being a friend for the time being, if you don't mind – I mean as far as my colleagues are concerned.'

'Let's say you've known me for some time, nice and vague,' said Emma, who could guess where this was going. 'I'll tell them I was living there between flats – and it's actually true, the bit about why I was living there, I mean.'

'We'll let them find out we're a couple later on. Not that it's any business of theirs, but for today we'll just say we've known each other for a while. I can't have them think I'm getting crime victims to have sex with me, I'll be up on a misconduct charge.' They looked at each other and laughed.

Sandra was a tall, skinny woman with an amazing asymmetric haircut that Emma couldn't take her eyes off when they were introduced. It looks as if it was created from a geometric drawing, she thought, she must have naturally totally straight hair, or it wouldn't work.

'Come through to an interview room,' said Sandra. 'Would you like coffee?'

'I do,' said Ben straight away. 'What about you, Emma? And Sandra? OK, I'll get it.'

Sandra asked no questions until Ben was back in the room, which struck Emma as quite sweet, but presumably most people would be devastated in her situation and need their support person. She decided to relieve any concerns Sandra might have right away and said, 'It's not as bad as it sounds — I was only living there very temporarily. I had to leave a flat I've been in for a couple of years and the one I'm moving to wasn't available straight away. I had nothing of value in that container, just what I needed for short while.' Basically, the truth, she thought, just a bit sanitised.

Ben came back with three disposable mugs balanced between his hands and put them on the table before he closed the door and sat down. 'You said you knew it was arson. Have forensics said how it was done?'

'Petrol,' said Sandra. 'They would have smashed the glass in the door first, then poured petrol all over the wooden floor inside — we could see a curtain rail above the ranch-slider so the curtain would have gone up in flames straight off.'

'If they smashed the glass they could slide the door open,' said Emma thoughtfully. 'From inside it's just little catch that you twist to unlock it. And then all they needed to do was put everything that would burn in a pile — my table, the armchair, bedding, my books.'

'Exactly,' said Ben. 'So, arson of the container and the car is one thing, but when you hear what happened a few days earlier, you'll realise that Emma might be able to point you straight at those who did this. and you'll be able to add another few things to the charges.'

They both looked at Emma and she took a quick

drink of her coffee, thought fast and said, 'It must be the same guys, of course - but setting fire to the container means they've not given up on me. It feels very scary.' She turned to look at Ben. 'And don't forget I still don't know why they came after me in the first place. I mean, they turned up at the river as if they were looking specifically for me. And now the container, the same thing – it's personal. I think it must be a case of mistaken identity.Maybe I look like someone they've got it in for.'

Sandra was just about to say something, when Ben said, 'Turn the recorder on – you're going to love this one. Emma's got a special talent when it comes to numbers, and she remembers the rego of their SUV from the incident at the river. Plus, she can tell you about the tattoo on one guy's arm. I think you'll find these thugs pretty quickly. And if you're interested, she can also explain why the number one isn't strictly speaking a prime number.'

They left two hours later; most of the time spent on Emma telling the story about the event by the river and answering endless questions. When Sandra asked, she explained how she got home in what she hoped was a convincing way and just said that a man picked her up on the road on the far side of the river and very kindly took her back to her car.

'Who was it that picked you up?' asked Sandra.

'Not that it matters, but weren't you lucky someone came along when you really needed help? Not a lot of traffic on that road, I wouldn't think, particularly at that time of the day. You must have been in a dangerous situation by then, wet and cold.'

'I'd never seen him before,' said Emma. 'A very kind man, very concerned about how cold I was and how far I had to walk. Quite worried I was hypothermic − he turned the heating up high and it was pure bliss to sit there getting warmed up. I was so lucky he came along just then.'

Ben's eyes were gleaming with hidden amusement while he listened to this, and Emma was grateful that Sandra's focus was on herself and her dramatic story.

'But why didn't you report it right away?' asked Sandra at the end of the interview. 'I mean, serious threats, having to take such extreme evasive action − a very risky move that! And then you didn't call it in - why?'

'I know,' said Emma and tried to sound apologetic. 'I should have, but by the time I got home it was late and I was frozen and still wet, and totally exhausted from struggling so far through the bush. I felt as if I was about to crumble in heap on the floor. And I was going away early the next day, but when I got there I thought I'd wait until I was back here and come in and see you rather than talk about it over the phone. I found it very hard to talk about it a first − well, I still do. It triggers something inside my head if I really describe what it was like, nearly drowning and thinking of what those guys would do to me if they caught up with me. Some kind of after-shock, I suppose, but quite hard to deal with. So, I asked Ben to come in with me today.'

She looked down at her hands for a moment and added. 'I really do think I was in a state of shock. I've never been on the receiving end of violence before, and those guys terrified me. It was as if it was just business to them, you know, threatening physical violence and making demands. And I had no idea what they were talking about - telling me I had to keep my mouth shut and give them my phone. And when they told me what they would do to me! God, I'll never be able to forget the way they talked about brutality and death so calmly.'

She paused again, while Sandra sat silently watching her and added a final comment before Sandra said anything. 'So, the first thing I did when I got back was to call Ben, because I knew he'd know what to do. And then we went back to the container, and it had been burnt!'

As they walked back to the car, Ben said, 'I can't believe how many slightly less than truthful things I've heard you say to people today. I didn't think you had it in you, I really didn't!'

'Neither did I. I've never done that before – been so strategically evasive, I mean. It's an unexpected talent. I'm quite pleased with myself for managing to come up with a good reason, though basically true, for why I didn't report it straight off. Why didn't we think of how to explain that? Obviously that's one thing she was bound to ask.'

'Probably brain fog,' said Ben. 'Love and sex must have muddled my thinking.'

Chapter 24

That evening, Emma and Ben discussed what their joint strategy would be in relation to family and friends. The plan was slightly complicated by the fact that there were people in both their lives who already knew too much to believe what they now referred to as the official version.

'Look at it like this,' Ben said, counting on his fingers. 'You have three people who either know a bit much, or who'll be able to guess we're not being totally open. Your friend from the library is the first one – you might have to tell her a bit more, to make sure she can dampen down any undue interest at the library, if your name comes out or something triggers a suspicion when this hits the media. Then there's Fletcher, and I can't remember what you said you've told him already, some of it at least, so maybe you want him to know the whole story. And the friend you talked to in the French

Bistro, what's her name, Nadine – she must be told how it all developed afterwards. She was directly involved after all, I mean that incident in the bistro.'

Emma nodded. 'That's it, and I do want Fletcher to know. And some time in the future I'll tell mum. Not right now, because first I want her to get the official version and get used to all the changes I must reveal. And what about Ariana? Will she connect the dots about me and you asking her about hypothermia?'

'Bound to,' said Ben. 'It will take two seconds and then we're in for it. She's as sharp as a tack and never hesitates to ask embarrassing questions. She's quite ruthless when she wants to find out what's going on, which is most of the time. Maybe we'll have her and Fletcher over for a glass of wine and tell them the whole thing a bit later, then swear them to silence. Do we leave Kiri out of the story when we tell them?'

'I think so.' Emma tried to imagine what complications might arise from Ariana discovering what her fourteen-year-old had been up to. 'We know Kiri can keep a confidence, so we could tell her that Ari knows it all, and to never let on that she does too. She's smart enough to carry it off. I wonder what Ariana thinks Kiri and Jonty have been doing together, though.'

'He said at the start he was giving her lessons in how to be really secure online and Ari agreed it was a great idea.'

'I've changed my mind. It's too complicated and I

think maybe it's best not to tell Ariana anything at all,' said Emma after running through the consequences in her mind. 'If we tell too many people bits of the story we'll forget who we told what, and then we'll trip ourselves up later. Let's keep it simple. How about I just tell mum about you, nothing about anything else, and we tell Fletcher everything at a later date. We don't tell Ariana anything because that will make Kiri's life much easier. If her mother knows nothing they can't talk about it, and she won't risk saying too much.'

'OK,' said Ben without stopping to think, much to her surprise. 'I've just been thinking the same thing – it would make it harder for Kiri.'

Now Emma was sitting at the kitchen table in a wedge of midday sunlight from the window beside her, waiting for her mother to pick up her What'sApp call.

'Hi mum,' she said when her mother answered. 'I hope it's your lunch hour so I can tell you my good news?' She laughed. 'I don't really know where to start, but the most important thing is that I've found the perfect man.'

'Really?' said Emma's mother. 'Is there such a thing? But if you have, congratulations! Tell me all about him.'

Emma knew Ben could hear her from the living room and smiled to herself at what she felt certain would follow. 'Well, let me get the demographic data out of the way first. His name is Ben Murphy. He's thirty-nine years old, born here, fully employed. And he says he will look after me forever. How's that for a start?'

She put the phone on the table and flicked her finger over the speaker button, so Ben would hear her mother's reply, and she knew exactly what his face would look like even though he had his back to her.

'Very exciting!' Her mother chuckled. 'What does he do? Has he been married before? Does he have children? Tell me everything, please!'

'I've known him for a while,' said Emma. 'He's just gorgeous – the kindest, most reliable man I've ever met. But we've just recently decided to live together, so I thought I'd better tell you and dad. I'll call dad later today. Ben has one ex-wife he's still friends with, but no children and a lovely extended family. Oh, and he's a police officer.'

'What a pity you had to give up your flat – you could have lived there together,' said her mother. 'It was plenty big enough for two and so nice and new.'

'Ben has a lovely house, and I'm moving in with him. Well, to tell you the truth I've kind of moved in already. We just have to shift some furniture and get rid of the excess stuff and then it's organised.'

'Send some photos, please, so I can see what he looks like.' Emma heard a voice talking in the background and her mother said, 'Sorry, I have to go, darling – someone's here to tell me something about the route trackers. Talk later – bye!'

'What does your mum do?' asked Ben who had appeared in the doorway. 'And thanks for saying nice things about me.'

'What did you think I'd say? Tell her you beat me up every Friday night and didn't feed me? I just told her the truth, that you're the most wonderful man I've ever met. Mum works for a large transport company – she's in charge of freight logistics and all kinds of things. Dashcams, mileage trackers, goods security and God knows what – mostly stuff I have no idea about how it works.'

On Sunday morning Ben got a slightly cryptic text message from Jonty. He studied it with a thoughtful frown, then passed his phone to Emma, who was sitting in her sofa corner with a physics textbook on a cushion on her lap, pad and pencil beside her. 'See what you think about this – I'm not sure I understand what he means.'

'*Draft blogs arrived from Dreadnought and Cosmos, very good, will print out for you to read. OK if I come over now?*'

'They're bloggers,' said Emma, handed his phone back and picked up her own. 'I've heard about them, but I've never read what they write. I'll check it out on the web. I don't follow stuff like that, though maybe I should - and I think they're both influential. Working in a library you're on the receiving end of random bits of information all the time. People talk to you and bring up things you never heard of, and I've heard those names several times.'

Ten minutes later she looked up from her phone. 'Huge!' she said and laughed. 'Both of them have massive number so followers on Twitter and Instagram and probably elsewhere – and on their websites. Check it out for yourself. If you search by their names you'll see endless quotes from regular news media about things they've said. They're obviously reliable. This is good! Whatever they write will get picked up.'

'But why did they send drafts to you?' asked Emma when Jonty turned up an hour later with Kiri in tow.

'She sticks to me like glue,' he said when Ben let them in. 'I texted her too, and she was tossing her bike in our front garden twenty minutes later.'

'I had to see it right away, of course,' said Kiri, whose fringe had changed colour from brilliant red to vivid green. 'You didn't expect me to first be useful and then just check out and forget about it, did you? And it was on Jonty's super safe computer, of course, that's where his anonymous email account is, so I knew he wouldn't forward it to me.'

As before, they sat in the kitchen and while Jonty opened his satchel and put a pile of printouts on the table Ben said, 'So, why did those bloggers send drafts to you? Don't bloggers just fire stuff off, like they don't care if it's true or not?'

'Not these two, not something as potentially explosive as this, when they don't know where it came from, remember I've not revealed who I am - but also because of some conditions I laid down. I gave them a couple of hints, so they'd start looking for more details, and then I said I might give them more later on if they promised to show me what they were going to publish before it went public. I hinted at a major discovery that would make their revelations go off like a bomb. Just to hook them in and get them to do what we want, and much to my surprise it worked.'

He turned to Emma. 'And we could maybe string it out a bit, do some more research and feed it to them bit by bit, so they continue blogging about it. We probably won't find anything they won't find too, but that's beside the point, it looks good. I've got a couple of titbits for them that I've held back for now, though – and then last of all that really major surprise they'll never be able to find for themselves.'

The room was totally silent while they read the printouts Jonty handed them, and the silence stretched out as one by one they put the sheets of paper down and stared at each other, then Emma said, 'This is brilliant!' at exactly the same moment Kiri shouted, 'O for awesome!' at the top of her voice.

Jonty and Ben looked at each other and grinned,

and Jonty said, 'Where the hell did you get that from, it's ancient, from way before you were born.'

'My English teacher says it sometimes — A for Apple, O for Awesome, she says, I think it's funny.' She picked up the printout again. 'Do you think the TV news will do a thing about this?'

'Definitely, and the newspapers. You probably don't know what newspapers are, but it's like the online news but printed on paper.' Jonty ignored the snort of derision from his niece and bent to get something else from the satchel at his feet. 'And I printed some posts from that hidden online website the Brotherhood has. I think one of them is about you, Emma. It's the one from a Brotherhood member whose online name is "nomercy88" that I've marked in bold. You know about the 88?'

The others looked blankly at him, and Kiri said, 'I did notice it here and there when we were searching — what does it mean?'

'The letter H is the eighth letter in the alphabet, and HH stands for Heil Hitler. It's very popular, particularly on far-right social media accounts and on that website the Brotherhood runs — they add it to their names.'

They read it together with Kiri leaning over Ben's shoulder to see the one Jonty had marked: *No reports of anyone drowning or missing, but the firestorm is coming.*

'If you tell them about the container and the car and all that, I'll make coffee,' said Ben.

'All of it?' asked Emma, making sure he meant what she though he meant, that she should tell Jonty and Kiri literally everything, because so far he was the only person who knew the full story behind her decision to live in the container.

'If you're ok with it,' said Ben. 'It's the last piece of the story that binds it all together and they deserve to know. And it explains the comment about the firestorm coming.'

'It's not that I don't trust you,' said Emma to Jonty and Kiri who were looking at her expectantly. 'It's just that it was kind of sad and depressing for me, so I've not really told anyone the whole story – apart from Ben, of course.'

She told them everything starting with the letter about the rent increase, how it coincided with her sacking, and the effect it had on just about everything in her life, from where and how she lived, to the kind of job she managed to get. Jonty and Kiri sat silently listening, their expressions changing from sad to outraged to fascinated. She had already told them a few days ago about the incident at the river and that Ben picked her up on the road, so she picked up the story from there but skated over the rest of that night, how he sat for hours watching her sleeping, making sure she was all right and her agreeing to go with him to his place the very next morning. Too private, she thought, too precious. It's just for us two. She could tell from Ben's glance at her that he understood the omission and realised they already had an unspoken shorthand way of communicating, which seemed as amazing as all the rest, as if weeks of normal development and getting to know each other had been concertina-ed into less than a fortnight.

But the revelation of how she and Ben had gone back to the container and found both it and car burnt, prompted a stream of questions, and Ben intervened. 'Drink your coffee and let her finish!' he said. 'Stop your mouths with a few biscuits and listen to the end of this drama – there's more to come.'

So, Emma added the details of the conversation with Arnold and the interview with Sandra and finally stopped talking.

'It'll be way too late for them to try to silence Emma when all this hits the media,' Ben said comfortably. 'The date of that firestorm comment you printed out is the day before the arson, so that's great to have, and now she's living here - no way can they find her. They'll be in deep shit very soon, so the threat to Emma is past its use-by date.'

'Good thing I downloaded that video clip from that website then,' said Jonty. 'They'll probably remove it now, try to protect themselves as soon as they realise the police know who they are, or very nearly. I'll send it to the bloggers – TV news will love it.'

They all looked at him waiting for more, and finally Emma said, 'Video clip? Of what?'

'Oh, sorry, I wasn't thinking – maybe I never told

you. It's the thing I'm holding out as the final bait for those two bloggers to do what I ask, that special thing I promised I'd give them if they complied with my demands.'

He grinned at Kiri, who was staring at him in disbelief. 'I was keeping it as a surprise for you too, Kiri. It's dynamite! It's a clip from a dashcam, and it shows those guys walking towards you, Emma and kind of boxing you in on the riverbank, grabbing you by the arm, and then you throw yourself into the water and swim across that little calm bay to where the current grabs you - and it rolls you over and then it pulls you right under and you disappear.' He looked across the table at Emma and shook his head slowly from side to side in disbelief. 'It's a powerful moment, it shows the terrible risk you took to get away from their threats. And then nothing, just those guys walking back towards the car, talking as if nothing's happened, facing the camera as if they're invincible, no attempt to conceal their faces. It's very dramatic. I think they recorded it to show off to the Brotherhood on that secret website. One of those guys uploaded it to the website and I copied it, but I'm prepared to bet it's gone now.'

'Jesus!' said Ben. 'Sandra's already got the rego of their car, but I must make sure to point out the video to her when it appears in one of those blogs or media— it's the best evidence she could get. Does it show Emma's face?'

For a long moment Jonty's forehead creased as he

thought, then he said, 'No, I don't think so – just your back and then when you're swimming, before the river grabs you, it's just the back of your head. Why do you ask?'

'If those guys confess when they're interviewed, then there's no need for Emma's name to get out. On the other hand, if they plead not guilty there will be a trial and Emma is the key witness. We'll have to wait and see. But it would be hard to plead not guilty when they're on video, because the attack at the river leads on to the arson via that firestorm post, so there's a clear sequence to link those events.'

That night over dinner, Ben held his wineglass up in a toast. 'We've already agreed we are the perfect couple, the Puritan and the Prude, but I have to make a really boring rule. No wine for me on weekdays unless we have visitors – but you can drink all you want.'

'I never drink on weekdays anyway, not unless it's a social occasion,' said Emma and looked affectionately at him. 'So, no problem for me. This last week has been the great exception – one long special occasion with wine every day.'

Chapter 25

On the Monday morning, one national newspaper's website quoted the blogger Cosmos, who had written a Sunday blog about the Brotherhood, quoting things from what he referred to as a 'supposedly private and locked website which contains explicit neo-Nazi and white supremacist content and seems to incite violence'.

By Tuesday morning all major papers quoted the bloggers' report on the container fire and again mentioned the Brotherhood post "nobody reported missing or drowned, but the firestorm is coming". On Tuesday evening the TV news played the video clip of the river incident, linked it to the firestorm comment and said it had come from the Brotherhood website but had since been taken down.

Overnight between Tuesday and Wednesday the entire Brotherhood website was taken down, but not before it was stated as fact on the RNZ news that the whole site and all its content had already been downloaded by the police as evidence of incitement to violence, and that it was to be used in a serious case currently being investigated.

On Wednesday afternoon police arrested two men and charged them with assault, threatening to kill, incitement to violence and arson.

On Thursday morning Sandra called Ben and asked him to bring Emma in to formally identify the two men in the video from photographs, and from there it snowballed, unstoppable and with increasing intensity. First by the revelation of the link between Gerald Miller and the Brotherhood, then that Miller's grandfather senior had been involved in founding the Brotherhood, which was news to Emma and Ben, but as she said, 'Sounds reasonable - he was already involved in 1991 when he wrote that letter, before everyone had the internet, so he might well have been the one who started it. Maybe with his friend Hermann.'

On Friday night Jonty called and told them that multiple people hiding behind aliases on the Brotherhood website and on social media had been identified by him and the bloggers, and the information would be written up in upcoming blogs, which would then inevitably be quoted by mainstream media.

. . .

On Saturday, when Ben and Emma were on their way to Ariana's for lunch, they heard on the midday news that Gerald Miller had been revealed to have multiple online identities and that he not only had a presence in the guise of different individuals on various far-right social media account, but in many places and under many names. The reporting detailed how Miller used his several online identities to praise himself for his sound and rational attitudes to promote himself as a great candidate for the Auckland mayoralty. As the presenter sarcastically said, 'Mr Miller appears to have a serious multi-personality disorder, or possibly a crowd-personality disorder.'

'It's done,' said Emma. 'We're of no interest now, we're mere specks of dust in a corner. What a nice feeling!'

For the last couple of days Emma had felt quite nervous at the prospect of meeting Ariana, but when she confided this feeling of anxiety to Ben, he just laughed.

'But why? I've looked really carefully at the video from those guys' dashcam and there's no way you can be recognised, if that's what you're worried about. Jonty checked the video again before he sent it and your face was visible very briefly when you turned your head to look at those men arriving, so Jonty pixilated it before he sent the clip to the bloggers.'

'So, we just say we've known each other for quite a while? And you've kept it quiet for some reason?

Because getting to the stage of living together in less than a fortnight will make them think we're mad, won't it?'

Ben looked carefully at her, as if he was trying to figure out just how worried she was. 'They're used to me keeping my private life to myself. Kiri won't talk, but Ari will try to dig under my barricade and find out where we met and stuff like that. Where *did* we meet?'

'Outside the French Bistro,' said Emma. 'On a Friday in February. You were on some kind of police errand, and I tripped on the famously uneven paving and nearly fell over, and you saved me from toppling. It does happen on that street and several people have complained about the paving on social media, and they come into the library and tell us about it – it's gossip central.'

'OK, that's sounds good. Let's stick with that story and if you supply the details Ari won't home in on me.'

An hour later, with all of them around the lunch table, Ari asked exactly the questions Ben had predicted, and Emma said without even glancing his way, 'Oh, it was the most embarrassing thing. I tripped on those uneven pavers near the French Bistro that people moan about on social media and if Ben hadn't been just behind me I would have fallen for sure. And it kind of went from there.'

Kiri looked innocently at Ben. 'A few seconds later and you could have missed the chance, and someone else might have grabbed her!'

'Were you the very cold girl?' Ariana wasn't finished yet. 'Ben rang one evening really worried about someone, he said he was concerned about hypothermia – was that you?'

'It was,' said Ben. 'She got soaked on a hike up the valley behind where great-aunt Annie lives. She didn't want to be inside, so while I was having coffee with Annie and fixing her kitchen tap, Emma set off for a walk on that track we used to ride our bikes on when we were kids. But it started pouring while I was sitting with Annie, hosing down – and you know how fast the creek up that track can rise, but Emma didn't, so she didn't turn around soon enough. She tried to wade across and fell in. We had the heater in the car up high, but she was seriously chilled.' He reached across the corner of the table and curled his fingers around hers. 'And then when we got back to Emma's place she fainted, so I called you.'

The rest of their visit went without any problems. Kiri's older brother Tama and Emma had instantly recognised each other from the library and spent a long time after lunch discussing what she was studying and what he was hoping to study.

'I was going to point out a book you might have missed last time you came in while I was still working there,' said Emma after they had covered the basics of their shared interests. 'I looked at what you had returned that day. I'm always nosy about what people read when we seem to have shared interests, but I missed you when you left.'

'I thought I hadn't seen you there for ages,' said Tama. 'Why did you leave?'

Emma hesitated for a moment, then said, 'They'd overspent their budget and had to reduce staff, and I was the last person hired, so I had to go.'

Ariana turned towards her and said, 'Have you got another job yet? No? Did you check out the health board's website?'

'No, I didn't even know there was a library there – is it for staff or patients?' She was surprised she hadn't thought of this earlier, but it had never occurred to her.

'It's a staff facility,' said Ariana. 'For research and info mainly - we subscribe to research journals, all kinds of medical science things. You'd be perfect, I would think – science and librarian skills.'

As they drove home late in the afternoon Emma said, 'I'll check the health board website as soon as we get home – I might be able to put my name down for next time they have a vacancy.'

Ben made no direct comment, and she wondered what he was thinking, but by now she knew that if she didn't ask, he would finish thinking, or maybe wait for the right moment, and then he would tell her. It became clear after dinner when he brought it up again.

'I don't know if this is the wrong thing to suggest,

and just tell me to butt out if I'm over-stepping the line, but I have an idea.'

Emma put her Kindle down and looked searchingly at him, alerted by something she hadn't noticed in anything she had heard him say before, he sounded nearly hesitant.

'Go ahead and tell me — it's not like you to shy away from things.'

'I'd like you to take the matter of the fake redundancy further, spend money on a top employment lawyer and light a fire under the person at the council who got you sacked. If a lawyer took it back to the Council's HR department, and if what's-her-name — Cora, isn't it? If she'd reveal who it was she was talking to that day when Anne heard her, then just the threat of a scandal might make them change their minds. Imagine if it was made public and if the link to the Brotherhood was hinted at. A top-level scandal, for sure.'

He paused briefly, but she said nothing, and he continued. 'That's presuming that you want to go back, but it seems to me you really liked working there, and it would be good for you to feel you won in the end, I think.'

'That's a lovely thought,' said Emma. 'And you're right, it would be good for my morale and maybe it would even restore my sense of justice. But I can't — the money I've got left from selling my good car isn't enough for that kind of lawyer. Not after using it for my living expenses for so long. I can't ask Catriona, because she would offer to do it for free, which I can't accept now they're having another baby or maybe two. I'll just look for something temporary until I can get another library job sometime in the future.'

'But listen - and I'm serious now,' said Ben. 'You might see this as interfering too much, but I've got money. I earn good money, I have savings and now I have you - and that's all I need in life. But I want you back on an even keel, and I want you to be happy. I'll pay for the lawyer, and until that's sorted out I don't want you to take some shitty job and earn peanuts. You should stay right here and study all day long. And then you can get the kind of job you want some time later when we've beaten the crap out of whoever got you fired.'

Six Weeks Later

Emma knew that Ben was watching her spreading peanut butter on a slice of toast. They were having a late breakfast on a Saturday morning when Ben wasn't working. 'Is that for me?' he said when she put the butter knife down.

'No, it's not for you,' said Emma and took a bite. 'I made one for you yesterday morning.' But she reached for another piece of toast and spread butter and peanut butter on it before she handed it to him. '*Why* is it that you always want the toast I fix for myself? I just don't get it."

'Because it's different from when I do it,' said Ben. 'It tastes different. No, don't laugh, I'm serious. I think it's the way you spread stuff, it's kind of bumpy and interesting. When I do it I get carried away and smooth it out too much and every mouthful tastes the same.'

'God. how I love you, Ben Murphy!' said Emma.

'You're unique – I was totally right from the very beginning.'

Emma's phone beeped a message alert, and she got up. 'It might be Ariana about those spring vegetable seedlings we talked about,' she said as she went to fetch her phone from the bedroom, then there was a long silence followed by a shout as she walked back up the hallway. 'Oh my God! It worked!' She held the phone out to Ben and watched him read the email.

'Right!' said Ben. 'Great result! The best we could have wished for. I was hoping that just the threat of action would work. Now we'll have to go out and celebrate again – let's go back to the lodge for dinner tonight if Fletcher hasn't got the place booked for some party.'

From: Vanessa Golding
Senior Employment Law Specialist
Morgan, Hodder & Golding
To: Emma Stewart

Hi Emma,

Good news just now after a closed emergency meeting held at the City Council last night. The person who arranged to get you sacked has resigned, and the finance department confirms there was no over-spend of the library budget. The job is yours again on the same terms, plus your salary from the date of your sacking to the present as a lump sum. Continuous employment record reinstated, and your four weeks' holiday entitlement also reinstated as compensation provided you agree to sign an agreement of confidentiality which binds you to never make the details public. The City Council will make a public statement to the effect hat "irregularities which caused an unwarranted redundancy at the library have been reversed".

Kind regards, Vanessa.

Many Thanks

We hope you've enjoyed reading this story and would consider leaving a review on your favourite review site, or with the retailer you purchased from.

These are not only much appreciated, they also help other readers discover new authors.

For more about other titles in this series, please read on.

Letters from the Past

Letters from the Past is a series of stand-alone novels where a letter from or about the past reveals something that changes a woman's perceptions of herself or of her family, and that affects her outlook on life.

These books are such fun to write, and I am always working on the next title in this series. I hope you will enjoy reading them as much as I enjoy writing them!

Tina

Having had nobody in her life since her husband died, Lara unexpectedly finds herself involved with three men. One is planning to use her, one she plans to use for her own ends, and one becomes a "friend-with-benefits" with surprising results. Sometimes a quiet schoolteacher is not all she seems at first glance.

Callista experiences an event of apparent ESP at the Okehampton Castle ruins and becomes a media sensation, but the effect it has on her life is dramatic. How do two people, one calm. one seriously claustrophobic, who feel they are poles apart, cope for an hour and a half in total darkness in a stalled lift? And can they handle the consequences?

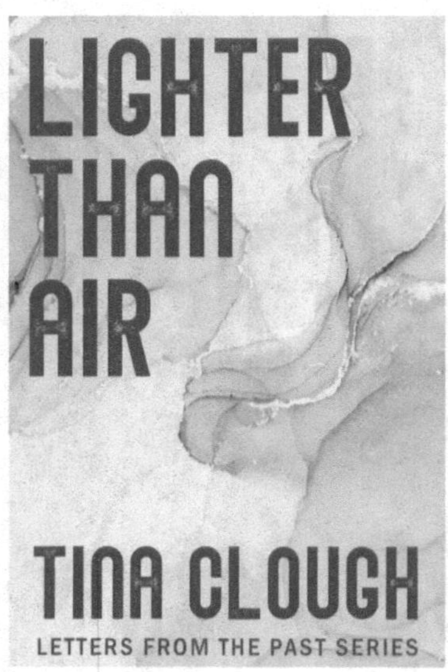

Sofia's life is in turmoil: a difficult diva mother, a letter with a confession about a family killing and having to accept help from a man she loathes when she is injured. Can reluctant attraction turn into love?

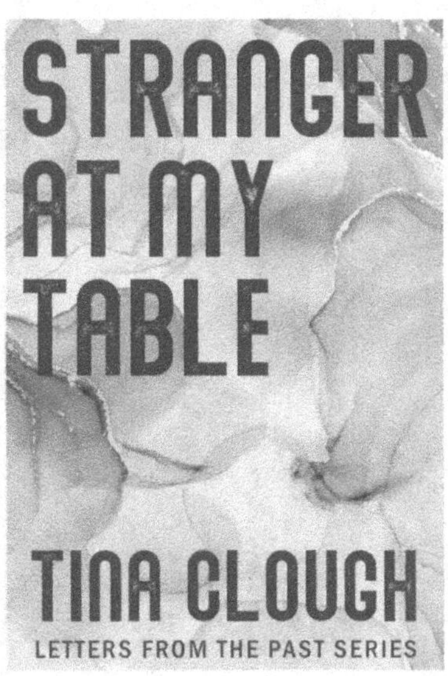

Who is the stranger living in the empty house Miranda inherited from her grandmother? Why is he living like a secretive recluse in someone else's house? Reckless Miranda decides to confront him, and what she discovers prompts her to set out on a fearless quest to bring justice to a man who has given up hope. But is the gamble too great or a risk worth taking?

When Emma finds an old letter in a library book she is instantly intrigued, but by researching the origin of the letter she unwittingly opens the door to danger and becomes the target for threats and harassment. Nearly desperate, she takes a leap of blind faith into the unknown and accepts an offer of help from a stranger - but can she trust him?

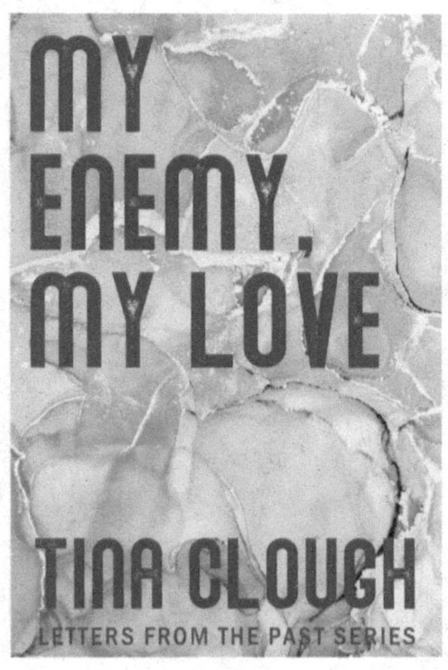

Jamie, an ardent protester against the gigantic Vista Resort development and Leo Masters, the high-powered developer, seem unlikely to ever agree on anything. But unexpected coincidences and chance brings them together in a fragile state of mutual respect. Will courage and kindness resolve the situation, or do they need help?

After a bizarre accident with ESP overtones, the media haunt Arapera. But can she trust an offer of help from a man she has only met once? Or will she regret it for the rest of her life if she doesn't take the chance? Sometimes life is a knife-edge balance between staying safe and taking risks, and there is no way of predicting if the gamble is worth it.

When crime-writer Saskia finds an unconscious stranger, she has a strange and strong emotional connection. Pretending to be his cousin and with no thought for the consequences, she spends weeks at his hospital bedside. But what will happen when he wakes and discovers she has invaded his life, breached his privacy and made crucial decisions on his behalf?

RUNNING TOWARDS DANGER

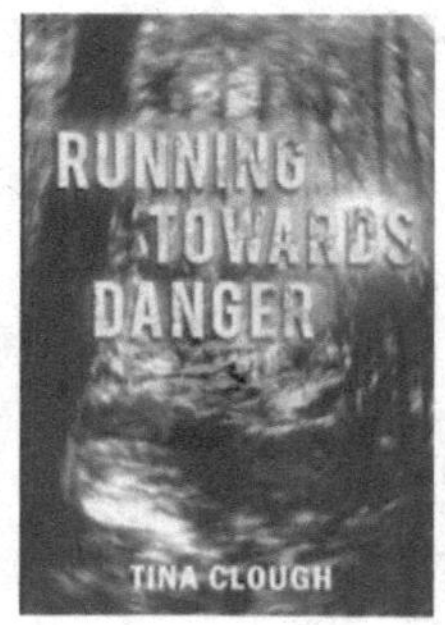

When Karen's flat-mate Nick is gunned down in front of her in the street her life is turned upside-down. Everything she thought she knew about him turns out to be a lie. She becomes a suspect in the police investigation and drug bosses think she knows where Nick has hidden a large sum of money. When her life is threatened, she decides to leave town and disappear.

Karen becomes Cara and creates an anonymous existence, severs all links to her past and adopts a cash-based way of life that leaves no electronic traces. But despite her careful planning danger still stalks her and she is forced to make dramatic choices in the face of threats and brutal violence.

Can she trust the man she is attracted to, or has he been sent by the killers to gain her confidence and find the money they believe she has?

THE CHINESE PROVERB

Book 1 - Hunter Grant Series

Army veteran Hunter Grant thought he had left war behind in Afghanistan – a conflict that left him with physical and psychological scars.

But finding an unconscious girl in the Northland bush and gradually untangling her story involves him in warfare of a different kind in his own country.

Hunter sets out to find and punish the man Dao calls Master, but he soon finds there is more to this story than enslavement. Before long he himself is being hunted by the overlord of a drug empire whose sole objective is to kill Dao because she knows too much.

Protecting her and waging war while trying to keep the police from stifling his enterprise takes all Hunter's ingenuity and determination and puts him in deadly jeopardy.

ONE SINGLE THING

Book 2 - Hunter Grant Series

Journalist Hope Barber disappears two weeks after returning to New Zealand from an assignment in Pakistan, leaving her front door open and her bag and phone inside. The police are tight-lipped about their reluctance to act, and Hunter Grant and Dao agree to help Hope's brother Noah find her. Details about Hope's time in Pakistan gradually emerge but only raise more questions.

Was Hope under surveillance?

Was she linked to terrorists?

And who is the man Hope called 'my stalker'?

FOLDED

Book 3 - Hunter Grant Series

First notes asking for help and folded into tiny origami shapes are found outside a city apartment building, then a physics textbook with tiny writing between the lines and then the woman who found them abruptly resigns and disappears. Are the notes asking for help real or is it a game? Hunter Grant, ex-army and with a pragmatic view of justice, reluctantly agrees to help find the missing woman.

Things get complicated when a high-powered lawyer arrives form the US, and shortly after his meeting with Hunter and Dao, a "cease and desist" letter arrives from the Cayman Islands. Inspector Bakker - a woman, who in Hunter's words "looks as if she would be useful in a brawl, provided she was on your side" - takes instant exception to his involvement and threatens to arrest him for interfering in an investigation.

Dao sets out alone on a dangerous mission, driven by a compulsive need to find out what has happened to the girl who wrote the notes, and Hunter looks death in the face when he decides to risk everything to put an end to the Darknet forces that threaten their lives.

THE SHADOW BROKER

It is 2026 and individual freedoms are severely curtailed, with state surveillance everywhere. State Security has a Watch List, and being on it means that nothing you do or say escapes the authorities, but does the Kill List really exist? And if it does, how would you know if you were on it?

Coded messages on a found burner phone, top-level government corruption and a shadowy mastermind who calls himself The Broker. In this climate of state control, three unlikely friends start quietly looking for connections and set in motion a deadly game of hide and seek that will change their lives forever.

Trying to uncover the truth means risking your life, and nothing is more dangerous than searching for evidence of government corruption.

About the Author

Tina Clough grew up in Sweden and now lives in New Zealand; dividing her time between writing fiction and translating and editing medical research papers.

Between working and writing she looks after an acre of fruit trees, vegetable gardens and roaming hens.

Apart from reading her interests include photography, wine, growing organic vegetables, making jam and kayaking.

https://lightpoolpublishing.com